# ROCK TO DEATH

In Gibraltar, Jack Scott finds a corpse — after seeing Nick Skaill walking out of a nightclub with a gun in his hand. But from the moment he informs the police, his life is in danger. Skaill's father is criminal Ronnie Skaill, a Briton living in Spain, who now wants to remove the only witness to this crime. Meanwhile, Liverpool detective Mike Haggard suspects Scott's brother, Tim, of a double murder. Bizarrely, the case suggests links to the Skaills. As Scott struggles with the puzzle's growing complications, there are more murders — followed by a bloody climax on Gibraltar's rocky slopes.

*Books by John Paxton Sheriff*
*Published by The House of Ulverscroft:*

A CONFUSION OF MURDERS
THE CLUTCHES OF DEATH
DEATH SUSPENSE
DYING TO KNOW YOU
AN EVIL RELEFCTION
LOCKED IN DEATH

JOHN PAXTON SHERIFF

◆

# ROCK TO DEATH

*Complete and Unabridged*

**ULVERSCROFT**
*Leicester*

First published in Great Britain in 2011 by
Robert Hale Limited
London

First Large Print Edition
published 2012
by arrangement with
Robert Hale Limited
London

British Library CIP Data

Sheriff, John Paxton, *1936* –
Rock to death.
1. Gibraltar- -Fiction.
2. Detective and mystery stories.
3. Large type books.
I. Title
823.9′2–dc23

ISBN 978–1–4448–1104–9

Published by
F. A. Thorpe (Publishing)
Anstey, Leicestershire

Set by Words & Graphics Ltd.
Anstey, Leicestershire
Printed and bound in Great Britain by
T. J. International Ltd., Padstow, Cornwall

This book is printed on acid-free paper

For my beloved wife,
Patricia Ann, gone now,
but loved always, and forever.

# Author's Note

As always, I have taken the liberty of tinkering with the geography in various locations, and putting facilities where none exist. One example: local residents will know that parking a car in Gibraltar is always a problem; for Jack Scott and others, at several key moments in the story, that problem doesn't exist.

I have also made walking the Mediterranean Steps a much riskier venture than it is now. Refurbishments to the area in the first half of 2007 were financed by the Bonita Trust and undertaken in conjunction with the Gibraltar Government who provided the management team in collaboration with GONHS. Safety has been greatly improved, and a site of biological interest and an area of outstanding natural beauty will be enjoyed by the public for many years to come.

But not, unfortunately, by Ronnie Skaill!

# prologue

It's almost midnight when you cross the deserted main road, jog silently across the grass verge and hard-packed sand and into the park. Heavy rain has slackened to a fine drizzle. Long wet grass whispers against your shoes as you walk through the dripping trees and look ahead towards the big field.

The fairground arrived in Liverpool a week ago, and is due to move to another town tomorrow. Most of it is in darkness, but warm light glimmers in the windows of several of the surrounding caravans and moonlight glistens on the wet canvas covering the coconut shies, the boxing booth, the .22 shooting range and the merry-go-rounds and waltzers and those places where you can throw undersized hoops all day long without winning a prize. And even at that distance you can detect on the night air the faint but lingering odour that is a sickly mixture of diesel oil, sawdust, candy floss and the fried onions the hot-dog and hamburger stands pack into greasy, dripping bread rolls.

At the edge of the trees, you stop. Your heart is hammering, your mouth is dry, but when you extend your hands and look at them they are steady. Steady, inside the thin black gloves, and very strong. A crooked smile twists your lips and you will recall, later, that it was at that precise moment — when you were still planning on using your fists to teach dark-haired Amanda Skaill a lesson she will never forget — that you remembered the knife. Remembered it, and realized that it was still in your pocket.

You drop your hand, feel the shape of the knife through the jacket's expensive supple leather. The jacket is a birthday present from your father. You were wearing it on the day the knife came into your possession. With the realization that it is there, with the hard *feel* of it telling you that you have not been mistaken, an idea flickers, flares, becomes so monstrous that you take a deep breath and literally shake yourself — though it is more a shudder than a shake — as if by shaking the rain from your jacket you can dislodge with it the thought that has burst into life and now refuses to go away.

And then you let your breath out explosively. Damn it, it's a good thought, a *good* idea. Probably the best idea you've ever had. Why dislodge it? Leave it there. Let it develop, let it grow as you walk, let it *ferment* you think, with a grin bereft of humour, for as

2

sure as eggs is eggs you know that in the flicker of thought that has already become an idea you have scarcely *touched* on the possibilities presented by the knife.

The fairground is a big one. As you set off again, you remind yourself that the attraction people call dodgems or bumper cars — depending on the degree of violence in their intentions when they sit down and grip the steering wheel — is smack in the middle. And that, you know, is where she will be. Amanda. With a lad called Tommy Mack, who lives eleven months and two weeks of the year on benefits but volunteers for work on the seven days in April and August when the fair comes to town. Specifically, he volunteers to work on the dodgems where every evening, time and again, in moves critically timed and executed with casual flair, he leaps onto each spinning or racing car in turn to collect the money.

Young Tommy is a poseur, you acknowledge, and you do so with a grimace because the lad's posing works. As Tommy leaps catlike from shiny floor to speeding vehicle, hanging on to the high pole with blue sparks flickering and crackling above his head, he makes damn sure he shows off not only his strength and agility but the tattoos that cover both muscular arms from shoulder to wrist like gloves of blue lace.

It works with an impressive number of impressionable young girls and, inexplicably, it worked with Amanda Skaill who surely can do better. *Had* done better. And there your face hardens. Because Amanda Skaill *had* been doing better, with *you*. All the way from April that year, as the asthmatic wheezing music of the fairground's steam organ faded away up the East Lancs Road, right through May, June and July until the music started swelling again — if not in reality then at least in the yearning shell-like ears of the impressionable Amanda Skaill.

She couldn't wait for the wagons to trundle into the park. Hadn't wasted any time, because you spot the two of them when you are some distance away. They are in deep shadow, at the end of the shiny arena in front of the operator's cabin where the dodgem cars are parked. A tall man with his back against an iron stanchion, the black T-shirt with sleeves cut off at the shoulders revealing his network of tattoos; Tommy Mack, the man who knows too much about you and what you have done; and the shapely, pony-tailed girl in jeans and loose blouse, hanging on to his bony shoulders with both hands as she nuzzled the hollow of his neck.

Tommy sees you as you step onto the track.

4

He ducks his head as he says something, grasps the girl's wrists. She turns, looks over her shoulder, then quickly steps away. She shakes off Tommy's hands. When you approach, you can see the light from nearby caravans reflected in her eyes. And there is uncertainty there that she is unable to conceal behind defiance you know is forced, and fragile.

She tilts her chin, stares boldly.

'What're you doing here?' she says.

'I came to check. I'd heard rumours, thought I'd make sure.'

'That's all they are. Rumours.'

'You say. But I knew already, didn't I? A friend of a friend. Where there's smoke. Shit sticks . . .'

But she's turned to Tommy.

She says, nodding her head at you, 'This is — '

'Your ex-boyfriend,' you cut in. And you raise your eyebrows, wait.

The tip of her tongue emerges to moisten glossy lips, and you know she is nervous. You have a reputation. So she is beginning to wonder.

'You don't have to be,' she says, mending fences, finger in the dyke. 'Not ex. Not permanent. You know? The fair leaves tomorrow. After that . . .'

'You think I like leftovers? Seconds?'

'You did before,' Tommy says, and his gaze is mocking. 'Loved 'em. After April you were right in there.'

'And now I'm not,' you say, but you are cutting him out and talking solely to Amanda. 'That's the way it stays, because it's finished, done, it's over.'

'Like that old Roy Orbison,' she says, watching him, reminding him.

'I suppose.' You smile. 'Anyway, that's my cue and I'll be pushing on.'

'Or pushing off,' Tommy says.

'Sharp, isn't he?' you say — and suddenly you are acutely aware of the knife.

Amanda gives Tommy a dirty look. She is less nervous, and becoming hopeful that a potentially dangerous situation is being defused. The fair does leave the next day and she is juggling all the clichés like *out of sight out of mind*, which will be Tommy, and *a bird in the hand*, which is a role she will submit to again, and yet again, if it will buy her time and hide her true intentions.

She flashes a bright smile.

'Do I get a kiss, then?'

'Thought you'd never ask,' you say.

You step towards her, your gloved left hand reaching out. You slip your arm around her shoulders. She comes warmly into your

6

embrace. Her right hand reaches the small of your back and pulls you into her. Her left comes up, cups the nape of your neck; ruffles your hair. You stand close, left cheeks touching. Her breath is warm in your ear, but you can feel the tremor in her body and know that she is steeling herself, trying valiantly for the Oscar.

'What's all this about boyfriend?' she whispers, nuzzling you. 'You shouldn't say that, not in front of people.'

'Well, you're a girl, I'm a boy — '

'Yeah, and as far as the world knows it's never been any more than that.' She puts a lot of intensity into her words, reassuring you. Her fingers walk like spiders along your collar.

Your left hand slides up. Your fingers close around her ponytail. She winces.

You say, softly, 'You told him, didn't you?'

'Who — ?'

'You know who. He's been acting different, watching me, something in his eyes. I think he knows. And who else could have told him? Not me. More'n my life's worth. So that leaves you.'

She hasn't told anyone, not yet, but quickly, desperate now, she whispers, 'Listen, how about I get rid of Tommy, you wait by the park gates?'

7

Your grip slackens. You squeeze her as if in agreement, look over her shoulder at Tommy Mack, and you wink conspiratorially because despite the harsh words you and he share several secrets. Then you begin drawing your right hand out of your pocket.

You have been holding the knife. It is a cheap Chinese import, a pocket knife, wood with brass ends, a curved blade. But, when folded, the very tip of the blade stands slightly proud of the wooden handle. As you pull the knife out of your pocket you let the exposed point of the blade snag on the material. It snaps open and locks.

Still holding her, you brace yourself then thrust the sharp blade in under her left breast and between her ribs. You hold it there, the handle hard against her, move the brass-bound end in a circular motion and visualize the point of the blade doing the same deep inside her body; deep inside her heart.

She gasps. Stiffens. Chokes. As she begins to sag you step away with the knife and grasp both of her shoulders. Then you throw her bodily. The top of her skull cracks against Tommy's face. She flops sideways, hits the floor hard. Tommy staggers back, hand to his mouth. He takes it away, lowers his eyes to look at the blood glistening on his palm; keeps them lowered a fatal second longer as he looks down in disbelief at the girl.

Without haste, you step over Amanda and slash Tommy's neck, slicing open his carotid artery.

Then, as blood spurts like a red fountain, you send the knife clattering and skidding across the floor, turn and jog away.

'Him and her,' you whisper. 'That'll teach them.'

But the man you are talking about, heady with triumph and the anticipation of what lies ahead, is not Tommy Mack.

# 1

## Monday

'I suppose you realize,' Sian said, her blue eyes thoughtful, 'that if we hadn't moved south to Gibraltar you wouldn't be in this mess.'

'We haven't moved south,' I retorted, pacing in front of her, away from her, forward, back. 'We've temporarily relocated — '

'Temporarily?'

'Temporarily, on a trial basis, relocated one arm of the business — '

'Eye.'

'What?'

Her eyes bore a roguish twinkle. 'You're a private eye, and that's the bit that's here. If it was an arm we'd relocated it would be like, well, the long arm of the law — and that's not us, that's more Haggard and Vine, your pet Liverpool coppers.'

'For Christ's sake,' I said, uncharacteristically short with her. 'The point I'm making is that the main arm, the toy-soldier business that makes the money, is still running smoothly back in the mountains of North Wales.'

'Of course it is. Calum's seeing to that.'

'But?'

'But we're here, running a security business — '

'Without any permanent commitment.'

' — while basking in Mediterranean sunshine, which would be absolutely delight-ful if you hadn't been and gone and put your foot in it.'

'Whatever.'

I swung away, avoiding her eyes as I did so because, dammit, I knew she was right.

* * *

By late evening there was still no news from DI Luis Romero of the Royal Gibraltar Police, and I was quietly fuming.

Three Islay single malts in the space of an hour had left me cold sober, but tension I couldn't shake off had created a headache that was an iron band clamping my skull. At eleven I automatically listened to the BBC's ten o'clock news, heard a two-day-old report on a double killing in Liverpool that was of no interest to me and switched off the radio. Acutely aware of Sian's presence as she drifted from kitchen to lounge, a blonde

12

ghost mocking me with her smile as I stalked the apartment casting furious glances at the clock, I finally stamped out onto the moonlit balcony. There I remained for the next half-hour, worrying, watching, only half-listening to the myriad sounds of a Mediterranean night: the soft rustle of the breeze through the tall, dusty palm tree alongside the balcony; the distant chirping of crickets; the lazy mosquito-hum of a plane on its curving flight path over Gibraltar Bay and the sudden explosion of sound as the pilot nursed it to a feather-light touchdown then applied reverse thrust to avoid plunging into the sea from the end of the tongue of land that was Gibraltar airport's runway.

Then, as startling as an electric shock, the telephone rang.

When I strode back into the apartment Sian had scooped up the cordless receiver and was holding it out, a smile on her lips that was both mocking and mildly apprehensive. I took it, rested a hand on her shoulder in a light touch that was a fleeting apology for my ill temper, then took a breath and walked away.

'Luis?'

I looked at Sian, nodded, saw the tightening of her lips.

'When? I was watching for the van. If you

didn't come this way you — ah!'

I nodded again, listened intently.

'And Ronnie?' I felt my lips twist at Romero's answer, uncertain whether to laugh or cry. 'All right. Thanks, Luis.'

I put down the receiver, met Sian's eyes.

'They've got Nick Skaill in a cell in Moorish Castle, charged him with murder. Luis Romero picked him up as he came across the border from La Linea half an hour ago, used an unmarked car to bring him in.'

'I think I saw it, coming up the hill.'

'But said nothing?'

Her blue eyes were direct, challenging. 'With you in that foul mood?'

I shrugged. 'So now it's up to Ronnie to make his move.'

'Oh yes. And he will, we both know that.'

'We knew it before I shopped his son. It was my choice — '

'Ours.'

'You accused me of putting my foot in it.'

'Doesn't mean I don't stand by your decision.'

'Anyway, it was my move, I accept the consequences.'

'Which are likely to be swift and violent.'

'Not necessarily.'

'Oh, come on!' she scoffed. 'You've pointed the finger. You're an eyewitness willing to

14

swear you saw Nick leaving the scene of murder, carrying a gun. When you stand in the witness box and testify, Ronnie Skaill's son will be looking at a life sentence.'

'Not just me. There could be other evidence, other witnesses.'

'No. Nobody else will have the guts to come forward, and by now the gun will be somewhere at the bottom of the bay. Without the weapon there'll be nothing to match to the fatal bullet, no fingerprints, no DNA. All the police have got is your statement. D'you think Nick's big, powerful father won't have thought that through? D'you think he'll let you get anywhere near a courtroom?'

'No. He'll stop me, if he can. But why risk a second killing? He might first try to buy me off. Do some kind of a deal.'

'There's no deal possible, and no point. As long as you're alive, his son's going to be looking nervously over his shoulder.'

'Mm. That's true.' I hesitated, nodding slowly. 'OK, Ronnie needs me out of the way so he's going to move quickly. The slamming of Nick's cell door will act like a starting pistol. Nasty men with guns could already be on their way here.'

'Maybe,' Sian said softly, 'you should have kept your mouth shut.'

'Or my foot out of it.'

15

I feigned uncertainty, walked slowly towards the balcony to hide a grin, gave her fifteen seconds then swung around to face her. The move caught her unawares. I stared at the flashing blue eyes, the thick blonde hair snatched back and gathered into a rough pony-tail by a plain elastic band, the thin white cotton blouse and the toreador pants stretched over hips that were so blatantly feminine they caused an immediate ache in my throat — and laughed softly.

For in her unguarded eyes I saw, not fear, not even apprehension, but the glint of a growing excitement. There was a touch of high colour in her cheeks, a quickness to her breathing.

'You've been looking forward to this, hoping it would happen,' I said. 'You can't wait to do battle, Soldier Blue.'

'My God, listen who's talking, it's you — '

'Me?'

She flashed a brilliant smile. '*Touché*. Us.'

'Right. New business, new location, new people to deal with and so inevitably new problems, and if we can't handle that — '

'Shh!'

Her urgent hiss stopped me. I turned swiftly, my head cocked.

We both listened to the laboured roar as a badly driven taxi rattled up Willis's Road. The

16

engine died with a wheeze. A door slammed. Footsteps scuffed on the road, on the stone stairs.

'Lord,' Sian said, 'he was quick off the mark.'

'That's not Ronnie. He wouldn't come in a taxi.'

'Maybe not Ronnie. But it would be convenient and anonymous for his thugs.'

I was no longer listening. I padded across the room, waited, then shot a glance at Sian as the approaching footsteps halted and the doorbell rang.

I wrenched open the door before the bell had stopped ringing, took one look, swore softly, reached for the heavy leather case that had been dumped on the threshold then stepped aside for the tall, dishevelled figure to enter.

'Jesus Christ, Timbo,' I said, 'd'you mind not coming at me out of the shadows like that? I felt the stab of pain, saw the long tunnel with the bright light at the end, knew for certain my heart had stopped — '

'Ignore him,' Sian said, stepping forward, '*Cardiac* arrest is not the kind that's bothering him. And Timbo must mean Tim, the long lost brother — right?'

'Tim, yes, but lost for any length of time is something I've *never* been.' With a quick grin at me and a wink at Sian, Tim pushed past and let his long stride carry him into the room.

Somewhat grimly, possibly thoughtfully, certainly apprehensively, I picked up his case and followed.

★ ★ ★

'So why are you here in Gibraltar?'

'It's September.'

'Which comes between August and October wherever you are. Your point being?'

'I always come here in September.'

'This year you had other plans. I'm babysitting, remember? Looking after your expensive canoe. El Pajaro Negro, the yacht that cost the bloody earth in borrowed money but looks shabby down there on the water amid all that obscene luxury.'

'My canoe,' Tim said stiffly, 'would not look out of place moored at Cap d'Antibes.'

'He's showing off,' Sian called from the kitchen. 'He's never been there.'

'The point is, you asked me to caretake.'

'No such word,' Sian said.

She came out to join us, carrying coffee mugs on a wooden tray which she placed on the table.

'It's what a caretaker does,' I said. 'And

18

Tim asked me to. Didn't you, Tim? So I've been making regular trips to the marina, checking the locks, pumping the bilges, charging the batteries, polishing this, oiling that — '

'Something came up.'

'I'm sure it did,' I said, glowering, 'and this is where violins begin to play as we head into the big confession. You're in trouble. I mean, isn't that a fading bruise I see on your noble forehead?'

'Was,' Tim said, leaning forward to pick up a steaming mug. 'Was in trouble.'

'Being here's not going to extricate you, Gibraltar's not a million miles from . . . ' I frowned. 'From anywhere, actually. But, look, one of the last things I heard about you was that you'd bought a peerage on the internet and become lord of a bleak rock in the Atlantic near the Outer Hebrides — and there's nothing out there to cause trouble but puffins and gannets and — '

'It's uninhabitable — and anyway, it was Liverpool,' Tim said, watching me as he sipped.

'What, you've got a peerage related to Liverpool?'

'No. That's where the trouble was.'

I groaned. 'Hell, I might have known. We move to Gibraltar to get away from mean streets and an even meaner cop called Haggard and — '

'And I *have* been there. Cap d'Antibes. I went there on the canoe's maiden voyage.'

'No, you didn't. The maiden voyage is what the canoe went on, when new, with Ronnie Skaill at the helm — because that's who you got it from, and that's who you're still paying.'

Tim looked guarded. 'Yes, well — '

'Is that true?' Sian jumped in, appalled. 'He got that bloody sardine can from Skaill?'

I grinned at the imagery and Tim's look of outrage, then grimaced and nodded.

'Mm, seems so.'

'But how do *you* know?'

'Eleanor told me.'

And now it was Tim's turn to look stunned.

'Oh my God,' he said. 'Where is Eleanor?'

'She's here, on the Rock. And if you want to know how she found out about your connection to Skaill, our dear widowed mother is living more or less permanently with an extremely rich and toffee-nosed ex-diplomat called Reg who's full of useless information studded with the occasional gem.'

'Tim,' Sian said, sitting opposite me and biting delicately on a shortbread finger, 'said 'Yes, well'.'

20

'When?'

'Seconds ago. You mentioned Skaill, said that's who he's still paying, and he said 'Yes, well'.'

'Christ,' I said. 'And that hesitation means you're *not* still paying, right? You've defaulted, and Ronnie sent a couple of his boys to sort you out. In Liverpool. That was the trouble.'

Tim nodded. He seemed to be waiting for me to fill in the blanks.

'There was a fight.'

Again the nod.

'In your flat.'

'Down at the Albert Dock, yes.'

'But you fought like a tiger, were facing defeat but managed to escape and ran like hell.'

He grinned.

'And this is where you ran to.'

'Right.'

I glanced at Sian, then back at Tim.

'You do know that, though born in Liverpool's Toxteth area — Lodge Lane to be precise — Ronnie Skaill now lives in Marbella and has got interests all over the Costa del Crime — plus here on the Rock?'

'Well, yes. As you pointed out, I got the canoe from Ronnie. But he doesn't know I'm here, and if I can lie low while I sort out my finances . . . '

'What you *don't* know,' I said carefully, 'is that I too am deep in the mire with Skaill.'

There was a heavy silence. A car clanked up Moorish Castle Road. Sian and I exchanged glances as we listened to it drive on by. The faint reek of petrol overpowered the scent of bougainvillea and warm sage to assail our nostrils. Tim was watching both of us.

'Go on,' he said.

'Skaill has a son called Nick. Without going into details, let's just say I heard a shot and saw Nick carrying a gun out of premises where a man lay dying.'

'And informed the police?'

'Mm.'

'Ronnie's son?' Tim said slowly 'Now that really is very interesting.'

'Why?'

He'd looked away, was gazing without seeing into the distance beyond the balcony's railing and the shiny leaves of the palm tree where a waxing moon shone on the glassy waters of the bay. Now he seemed to shake himself.

'Well, I mean, I'm in trouble, you're in trouble, and the common denominator seems to be Ronnie Skaill.'

'This fight with Skaill's hard men. Is that where the blood came from?'

'What blood?'

'You dumped your leather jacket on a chair when you came in.' I jerked a thumb over my shoulder. 'There's a big dark patch on one sleeve. I think it's blood, and now I'm waiting for you to convince me I'm wrong, or tell me, yes, it is blood, but there's a perfectly innocent explanation.'

Tim put down his mug with a bang. Suddenly his face was pale, his eyes avoiding mine.

'My, my, Jack,' Sian said softly, 'what have we got ourselves into this time?'

# 2

It was an hour later when I drove Lord Scott to the marina in an ancient salt-corroded ex-army Land Rover that was held together with green paint and a lot of rust. I'd bought it from a contact in the Royal Gibraltar Regiment. He'd got it for a couple of hundred euros from a building contractor who'd gone bust across the border in La Linea. British vehicle, carried bricks and cement in Spain, bought second-hand by a Gibraltarian corporal who'd probably laid a mattress in the back and called it a passion wagon, third-hand by a Brit — me — who was more accustomed to the power of an Audi Quattro that was now parked behind an old stone farmhouse in mountainous North Wales.

None of those thoughts had crossed my mind when, with great reluctance but very clear purpose, I volunteered to take Tim down the hill to his canoe. I had other things to think about, for I knew that even a single minute away from the apartment left Sian in danger. Nick Skaill was in prison, my testimony would ensure he stayed there.

There could be no better way for Ronnie Skaill to put pressure on me to retract than by kidnapping Soldier Blue and inflicting upon her all manner of torments. In the circumstances his methods would be brutal, I knew it, Sian knew it, yet still she waved me away with nonchalance in her stance and the devil of defiance dancing in her blue eyes.

Flaking white walls magnified the throaty cough from the vehicle's flaking exhaust as we made the rapid descent. The air was balmy, at first heady with the scent of bougainvillea, the peppery smell of sun-soaked geranium, the ripe sweetness of fallen oranges. Then, as we rattled along Line Wall Road, nostrils flared to the ranker smells drifting in from the sea and the evocative odours of tarred hemp and machine oil from nearby dockyards. High-rise apartment blocks and fancy restaurants reared giddily into the night skies from reclaimed land, but even they were dwarfed by the towering, floodlit north face of the Rock.

Then we were swinging in towards Marina Bay, before us in the moonlight the glint of flat water and a forest of gleaming masts sprouting from the gently swaying teak decks of a million dollars' worth of sleek power boats, catamarans and ocean-going yachts.

Legal parking on Admiral's Walk is as rare as those flecks of gold once found in the wet gravel swilling at the bottom of Californian prospectors' pans. I parked illegally. Slamming the doors, we walked quickly past Bianca's restaurant towards the concrete walkway at the centre of which *El Pajaro Negro* was moored like a predatory bird. Smoke from the Land-Rover's worn engine lingered like a blue haze.

On one of the moored vessels a champagne cork popped. It sounded like a distant gunshot. A ship's bell clanked, and a blonde female hung on to its rope and giggled drunkenly. She was wobbling tipsily under a rectangular canvas awning held up by four poles. Suspended lanterns swayed gently to the water's slight swell, creating moving shadows. Other girls in skimpy two-piece swimsuits were sprawled on loungers or hanging around the necks of brawny men in posing briefs. Heavy gold bracelets glittered, champagne glasses foamed onto the teak decking as a tall, white-haired man in faded jeans and a suntan poured champagne carelessly from a magnum. As we walked by he saw me looking across at him. His teeth flashed in a grin as he held the bottle high, waggled it, and lifted his other hand in an obvious invitation.

I smiled, and shook my head. He shrugged, turned away after what seemed to be a searching look and, as one of the girl's said something to him, he shook his head and ducked out of sight.

And then we had reached Tim's canoe. My caretaking days over I tossed him the cabin keys, watched him lug his suitcase aboard *El Pajaro Negro* and stand for a moment on the gently rocking deck as if stunned. Perhaps he was. He had acquired the canoe on a whim, now owed more money than he had any hope of finding, and the people chasing him were no ordinary bailiffs.

I didn't know the full story, but from what I'd scraped together it seemed Tim had bought the forty-foot vessel from Skaill when the crook had ambitions of creating a smuggling empire. I suppose swashbuckling Timbo had seen it as a romantic way of making a lot of money, Skaill content to hand over the tiller so that, as always, he was at least one step removed from the action should things go wrong. The Liverpool rogue had painted her a dull black so intrepid pirate Tim could elude coast guards, and christened her *El Pajaro Negro* because she was, Skaill swore, 'as swift as the swiftest of birds'. And I was convinced that from the very beginning Tim had worshipped her as much for her chimerical buccaneering connections as for the richly panelled cabin and the twin Merlin

27

diesels that powered her through the blue Mediterranean waters at a mind-numbing forty knots.

I let him go ahead, listened to the jingle of keys as he fumbled with the big brass padlock and the cabin door swung open. I followed, feeling my way. A switch clicked, and Tim was bathed in yellow light. He entered the white-carpeted salon and, as I moved in behind him, I was immediately conscious of familiar smells: teak oil, metal polish, stale perfume, the sweetness of bottled gas, and from the powerful engines tucked out of sight in the bowels of the vessel the faint but unmistakable reek of diesel oil.

Tim dumped the case and immediately snapped open a cabinet beyond the plush L-shaped sofa and began pouring drinks from a new bottle of Jameson's whiskey.

'What's that for?' I said, watching. 'Balm for bruising encounters done with or anticipated?'

'To oil my vocal chords. Sian fed me, fattened me up as it were, while you watched with a cynical eye. You certainly didn't ferry me down here out of charity. You want the full story — right, Jack? The hows and the whys and the whos. Especially the whos, because something I said hinted at a common enemy.'

28

'Now *that really is very interesting,*' I said, smiling faintly as I echoed Tim's earlier words. I sipped my drink, raised an eyebrow. 'You said that when I mentioned my troubles with Skaill. And guess what? I didn't buy your story.'

'There *was* a fight. I *do* owe him money. He *did* send along the enforcers.'

'I don't doubt it. But if you got away they must have been his second or third team, and that's certainly not when you got all that blood on your jacket.'

'You can't possibly — '

'My trouble involves Skaill's son, Nick. Your reaction, when I told you, was odd. Now, I know Skaill's also got a daughter. She spends her time in Liverpool. So, please, tell me you haven't got yourself involved with that young girl. Even better, tell me that what I'm thinking is pure fantasy: that your sleeve and Amanda Skaill's blood did not somehow get . . . intermingled.'

Tim chuckled.

'Intermingled?'

'As good a word as any. Just tell me I'm wrong.'

'You're right, but the story you've dreamed up is certainly miles away from the truth. Her blood intermingled with my sleeve when she was falling-down drunk outside a Liverpool club. Off Canning Street, up the hill from Paul McCartney's performing arts place.'

'Jokers Wild.'

'That's the one. She cut her scalp on a sharp door latch. I was the passer-by she clung to and slid down on her way to the wet pavement.'

A shriek of hysterical laughter echoed across the water. Then there was a sudden splash, a terrified squeal followed by a guttural oath.

'Man overboard,' Tim said softly, and I thought I detected an involuntary shiver.

I watched my tall, elegant brother hold his glass at a dangerous tilt as he clicked a switch on a built-in stereo unit. The opening of something by Dire Straits started in the muted way so many of Mark Knopfler's compositions do. *Telegraph Road?* I couldn't be sure. Then the deck moved gently beneath my feet as Tim crossed to gaze out of one of the portholes and for several moments we sipped the fine whiskey, the swelling music a pleasing background to unpleasant thoughts as we gazed at the lights of Gibraltar that formed a wide, glittering staircase climbing all the way to the stars.

'The way you put it,' I said, 'you make it sound as if that accident was the start and the finish of a quite ordinary evening out in a city

30

centre. But actually, it's never like that with Ronnie Skaill, is it?'

'He is under the impression I hurt Amanda deliberately,' Tim said, still with his back to me. 'An altercation that went badly wrong, something like that. Perhaps she gave him that idea, told him we had a heated argument and it turned violent.'

'What, you mean you were seeing her regularly? As in . . . well, seeing her?'

'Maybe. The point is, whether I was or I wasn't — '

'It's now not just about money.'

Tim shrugged, hesitated. Then he said, 'Did you notice those headlights? A car's just pulled in. A Merc. Black. It's parked close to Bianca's.'

'Lurking.' I nodded. The lights had swept across the moored millions, searchlights raking the walkways for a known target. Or was that fanciful at best, at worst paranoid?

'With Skaill after you there was no way you were going to slip into Gib unnoticed,' I said. 'That car probably followed you from the airport. Parked in Flat Bastion so the driver could see up Castle Road. Tagged on again when we came rattling down the hill in the rusty tin can.'

Tim took a deep breath. 'Let's go up top,' he mumbled, and without waiting for a reply

31

he swung away and made his way on deck.

Again I followed. He was leaning on the rail, gazing across at the dark shape of the Mercedes huddled against blond brick. I joined him, looked down at the water, then sideways at my brother.

'Tinted windows, hi-tech aerials that look as if they can pick up more than Radio Gibraltar. Mercs are not unusual, there's a lot of them on the Rock, and yet . . .

Tim glanced at me, his eyes lost in shadow. 'I've got a gun in the locker. If I need it. Dad's shotgun, he left it to me in his will. But you know that. It's the engraved Verney-Carron over-and-under.'

I sighed. 'You'll never use it. If you do you'll probably lose a foot.'

'Wrong, Jack.'

'Meaning I don't know you? We've been apart too long? Well, maybe. The point is, why put yourself in a position where you might be forced to start shooting? You owe Skaill money for this bloody canoe and . . . hang on, what about mooring fees, if you can't pay for the boat how can you pay those?'

'I don't. I think they're waiting for ownership to revert to Skaill, then they'll go cap in hand to him.'

I shook my head in despair. 'OK, so you owe everybody money and it's also possible

Skaill thinks you've been messing about with his daughter. If I'm right and he knows you've flown to Gib — and he's bound to — isn't this the first place he'll look? I mean, OK, maybe you did slip in unnoticed, maybe that Merc's innocent, didn't follow you. But I don't believe it. A phone call has alerted the heavies. Christ, they're probably slipping on the black leather gloves or the brass knucks as we speak. They're waiting until I drive away. Then they'll pounce.'

'Why wait? Isn't Skaill after both of us?'

'Your arrival has shot you to the top of the list. And I think Skaill will try talking to me, or apply a different kind of pressure.'

'You mean he'll lean on Sian?'

'Yes,' I said. 'But he also knows that she's not the only woman here, in Gibraltar, that I care deeply for — '

'We care for,' Tim said, and he swore under his breath. 'Dammit, Jack, what the hell have we done?'

'What we've done is past and cannot be undone. And I'll look after Sian and Eleanor. My immediate concern is your situation. You do realize those men in the Merc will be more ruthlessly efficient than the clowns sent to your Liverpool flat? They'll wait for the wee small hours when you're fast asleep and the cool mist is hanging over the bay and in that

33

half light they'll step aboard with the stealth of cats.'

'Let them,' Tim said softly. 'An Englishman's home . . .'

'Mm. Mortgaged to the hilt. But seeing that car has changed everything. I think bringing you here was a mistake. You should come back with me.'

'Mortgaged,' Tim said, 'but insured courtesy of a well-oiled 12 gauge.'

I made a soft sound of exasperation, swiftly drained my glass and placed it precariously on the cabin's curved roof.

'Do me a favour, Tim. If you're determined to stay and you feel jumpy, accept that rich character's invitation to the party. Hold your glass under his foaming magnum, carouse the night away and get yourself so well-oiled there's no way you can make it back to this death trap.' I suddenly remembered a recent news item, and smiled. 'You should be safe enough there. That gin palace was broken into recently, and once bitten . . . Well, actually, he'd left the door open. Thieves got onto the boat. Bottles of expensive booze were taken.'

'Really? I wonder how the robbers knew it was there?'

I chuckled. 'I know. It's a well kept secret, isn't it? Anyway, the point is the experience has probably made the owner security conscious. He's obviously rich, sure to have some kind of weapon on board, and I'd say you'll be safer there than almost anywhere.'

Tim was pulling a face, clearly not liking the idea.

'Well, all right, if that doesn't appeal to you then go below and get your head down. It won't keep those boys with the brass knucks away, but at least you won't see them coming, won't know what's hit you.'

'That's all right then,' Tim said with a wry smile.

'If it helps,' I said, 'for the next couple of days I'll stick to my caretaker routine. Only I'll be looking out for you, not the canoe. That means I'll see you early each morning. OK?'

'To make sure I'm still alive? Sure, I look forward to it,' Tim said, reluctantly dragging his eyes away from the silent black Mercedes.

I clapped him on the shoulder, glanced once into those tormented blue eyes, then jumped ashore and jogged the short way to the battered Land-Rover. I swung the rattling vehicle in a deliberately wide arc, passing close to the parked Mercedes. Through the tinted windows I thought I could detect what might have been the glow of a cigarette, the shine of sunglasses over dead eyes. But I was travelling too fast, being extra careful not to drive into the water, and it was impossible to be certain.

As I drove away from Marina Bay I took a last, anxious look back at *El Pajaro Negro*. Tim was standing at the rail, a tall, pathetically forlorn figure. He must have seen the pale oval of my face as I glanced from the Land-Rover, for he half lifted a hand, as if to wave, then let it fall to his side.

Then I was away, deliberately banishing the sight from my mind as I picked up speed and drove back towards the upper Rock. With me, like the beginnings of a dull, nagging headache, I took just about the biggest cock-and-bull story I'd heard in a long, long time.

# 3

'So what's the young fool done this time, Jack?'

The question she always asked. The one I was never sure how to answer.

The broad Liverpool accent was at odds with her appearance: she was tall and white-haired, comfortably elegant in a long cotton dress that fell with grace over her lightly-boned frame, its hem brushing soft Indian sandals. It was her preferred mode of dress, her favourite ensemble, she would say, with a mysterious smile and a flutter of long eyelashes as she twirled and glanced coquettishly at you over her shoulder.

I'd climbed the wooden steps of the tidy bungalow set high against the Rock's western slopes, knocked once and walked in through the door my mother steadfastly refused to lock. She'd taken one look at my face and cast her eyes to the ceiling in despair.

There was the wonderfully familiar, discreet scent of lavender as I grasped her shoulders, bent slightly to kiss her cheek; a firmness in her arm as she pushed me away that brooked no nonsense. In her hand there was a tall glass of gin and tonic with a slice of lime; her nightcap, without which she swore she couldn't sleep, and her brown eyes would laugh at you, dancing, daring you to argue.

I crossed the thick rugs covering the dry board floor to the drinks cabinet and poured Islay whisky she kept specially for me, turned to face her.

'Money,' I said quietly. 'He bought that boat, and now he can't pay for it. He owes Ronnie Skaill a small fortune. Which to Tim is a big fortune.'

'So what did they do? Beat him up then wreck his Liverpool flat, send him running for the first plane out here?'

'Is that what Reg reckons?' I cocked my head. 'Where is he, by the way?'

'Tucked up in bed. Dreaming of past triumphs and tragedies when diplomacy won, lost or abstained — or counting the latest profits from his investments. And, yes, that is what he reckons. Perhaps even knows for sure. He always seems to, bless him. Fingers on lots of pulses, some of them almost fatally erratic from clinging limpet-like to too many port decanters at too many dinners. But there's also a lot of people in positions of authority who delight in trickling the right information in Reg's direction.'

I watched her sit down on an old

38

*chaise-longue* colourfully draped with fringed blankets, this strong, independent widow who insisted her sons call her Eleanor yet who could be moved to tears by the simplest of gifts. The long ropes of dark beads looped about her neck rustled like dry palm leaves. The deep red shade of the table lamp on the low bookcase behind her transformed her white hair into shimmering cascades of glorious pink touched lightly with highlights of gold. Carefully contrived, I knew, designed to create a precise image by a woman who cared for her appearance, and the effect it had; in her Liverpool flat an identical red lamp worked the same magic.

'And now it's two of you,' she was saying, 'in Ronnie Skaill's bad books, and that really is a position of considerable danger. Tim's here, but he's not out of the woods so what's he going to do now? Sell the boat? Hand it back? Tell Skaill to go and take a running jump? Or offer that soft Scouse crook a quid a week?'

I smiled at the thought. 'Skaill may be getting old but he's certainly not soft, in the head or anywhere else. As for Tim, for now he'll do nothing,' I said, easing myself into a low wicker rocking chair and placing my drink on the loose rug. 'Mainly because he doesn't *know* what to do.'

'He should go and see Skaill, tell him to keep his hair on, he'll get his money only it'll take a bit more time.'

A statement. Nothing to it. Plain sailing. She rolled the half-empty glass between her palms, gold rings clinking.

'If he goes to see Skaill,' I said softly, 'you might never see him again.'

'I don't agree. One thing Skaill loves more than anything is filthy lucre. And Tim owes him.'

'I've told Tim to lie low,' I said carefully, 'told him I'll keep an eye on him.'

'Oh, come on, Jack. You can't do that twenty-four hours a day — and anyway, you know damn well Lord Silly Ass won't sit still for more than a few hours. He'll be up and prowling, he'll think up some crackpot illegal bit of nonsense for makin' money to pay off the debt and end up owing twice what he owes now.'

'Maybe.' I picked up my glass, tilted it, watched the malt whisky catch the light. 'But this time it could be different. He's scared, Eleanor. I think he will lie low, keep out of sight — though I did tell him he's chosen the wrong bolt hole.'

'The boat? Surely that's not where you left him?'

''Fraid so. Reluctantly, and with a feeling

40

of guilt. And now there's a black Mercedes lurking nearby. Sinister.'

'They all are, caught in the wrong light, wrong situation. So is that why he's scared? Or is there more? And don't lie to make it easier for me,' she said, catching my look. 'Because it won't. I need to know, Jack.'

'There's a possibility that he got involved with Skaill's daughter. He came to us straight from the airport. When he shrugged out of his leather jacket I saw bloodstains on the sleeve. He told me the girl — her name's Amanda — was drunk outside a nightclub, she cut her head and he happened to be there. The trouble is, it's possible the vindictive Miss Skaill told her father she and Tim came to blows. And if someone, anyone, has harmed a hair on his daughter's head we both know how Skaill will react.'

I finished my drink, rose from the chair and crossed to the wide window. Gazing out into the darkness I let my eyes follow a line that I knew led down the steep west slope of the Rock, down past the ledges and feeding stations at the Apes Den, across the sloping ribbon of Europa Road, beyond that the palms and shrubs of Alameda Gardens, Trafalgar Cemetery, and the twinkling lights of the town . . . the marina . . .

I heard the rustle of her dress, the whisper

41

of sandalled feet. Then her hands were on my shoulders. She turned me, shook me gently but firmly.

'Keep them to yourself, right, Jack, all the scary bits you discover when you're looking into this.' Her eyes searched my face, and despite the warmth of the room there was a coldness in them that almost caused me to shiver with apprehension. 'Because you *are* going to look into it. You're going to sort it out, this problem Tim's got with Skaill. And then you're going to sort him out. Tim Scott. Once and for all. Try to get his mind off the easy money, off even easier young women who'll wait until he's plastered then roll him. Or, like now, drop him in very deep and sticky — '

'Mire.'

'Yeah, right.' Her fingers were digging into my flesh, her smile unsteady. 'He's away so often, so long, we hardly see the young bugger, do we? And when we do, he's always brought home a backpack full of trouble.'

'He's your son, he's my kid brother — and he's a bloody idiot.' I reached up, grasped her wrists, looked into her eyes. 'Something's screaming at me that this time he's gone too far, and my mind's cringing at the possibilities. All right, of course I'll do my best to get him out of the . . . the mire, but you and I know I'll be battling against Tim as much as Skaill's mob.'

For a moment she leaned her forehead against my chest and I felt the faintest of tremors, waited patiently until she regained control. Then she took a deep breath, and stepped back.

'Whatever we do to protect him he'll lead us a merry dance, won't he?' she said and, although moisture glistened in the fine lines at the corners of her eyes, she was smiling and I knew that look expressed a supreme and perhaps misguided confidence in my ability to put everything right.

I grinned. 'Oh, yes. The hot sun will act like a soothing balm, the Levanter will whip those familiar wisps of cloud off the Rock's summit and create restlessness, both together will dispel the last traces of Tim's fear — and then, who knows?'

'Who indeed?' she said, and now I detected in her eyes the same flicker of excitement I'd seen in Sian's. Two women years apart in age but cast from the same mould? Probably. Yet even as the thought crossed my mind those eyes had changed again and were once more focused intently on me.

'So with him out of the way, Jack, with him sorted, now it's over to my favourite PI's problems, because you've been and gone and put your foot in it.'

'Shopped Nick Skaill. Couldn't have made things any worserer.'

'So now it's a balancing act, then. You tread the fine line between helping Tim and putting yourself in danger,' she said.

'Fair enough, I'll watch my back. But we haven't mentioned Skaill's other options. Have you thought about those, what are they?'

'My imagination's flagging. You tell me.'

'I can think of two. They're called Sian and Eleanor.'

'Oh God.'

'Sian can look after herself, but I'm going to suggest she moves in with you and Reg.'

'I'd like that. Female company. Two of us should be a match for Reg, my lovely but eccentric and often trying diplomatic dip-stick. And this bungalow's safe enough, it's like an eyrie. Where eagles dare, and all that.'

And then my mobile phone rang.

★   ★   ★

It was DI Mike Haggard. Over the past few years, when taking time off from Magna Carta, my toy-soldier business, I'd worked on several crime cases in which he and DS Willie Vine had been involved. Now I glanced at my watch. Liverpool was an hour behind Gib, but still a call at this time meant Haggard was working late, and more bad news.

I sensed Eleanor watching me, knew she was having the same bleak premonitions without knowing who was calling, and politely turned my back.

'Ill Wind,' Haggard said, using the name he'd coined for me during the Gerry Gault case[1]. 'Thought you might be interested in the latest on those fairground murders.'

'I'm not sure I am. Calum phoned, gave me the bare bones of the story. Told me soaking up the Mediterranean sun would addle my brains, what I needed was the cerebral exercise of a juicy murder case. He could be right, but why are *you* phoning me? The last thing you want is me getting under your feet.'

'Maybe there's a connection.'

'What's that mean?'

'I'll get to it. But, first, a witness has come forward. Feller who runs the boxing booth. He was outside his caravan around midnight, peeing in the long grass. Says he heard voices, walked a few yards so he could see what was going on. He missed the action — '

'I'm still not sure I'm interested.'

---

[1] *A Confusion of Murders*

' — a girl stabbed, bloke with his throat cut. Both dead, place slick with blood. But all this feller saw was vague shapes lying next to the parked-up dodgem cars. Then he spotted a figure running away. Saw him because at that moment he was leaving the park and was caught under those sodium street lights. Tall, slim, this feller said. Wearing jeans, a leather jacket. Those lights are horrible, but the witness reckons black — the jacket that is, not the bloke.'

'And the connection?' I managed, as the blood in my veins turned to ice and a pulse began throbbing in my temple.

For a long moment there was silence.

Then Haggard said, 'On second thoughts, I'm not going to risk it over a mobile connection. So here's a better idea. It'll take you about three hours to get to Manchester. I suggest you catch the first Monarch flight out tomorrow.'

# 4

## Tuesday

The morning sun was turning 6000 feet of runway into a griddle hot enough to bake scones and I had just handed my boarding pass to the Monarch flight attendant at the top of the steps when my mobile phone rang. I acknowledged the attendant's stern warning glance and took the call quickly as I slipped into my seat. It was DI Luis Romero. He waded straight in, and his message was stark. Tim was in Gibraltar General Hospital. Half-sozzled guests staggering away from a yacht found him unconscious quite close to Bianca's restaurant. He was lying with his head hanging over the bloodstained walkway. He'd been badly beaten.

'Not life-threatening,' Romero said. 'But maybe the message in the beating is more to be feared than what has already come to pass.'

I asked him for the hospital's telephone number, jotted it down on a scrap of paper, then switched off. Unfortunately, switching off didn't rid my mind of his parting comment. The trouble Tim was in suggested the vicious beating had been a warning, the warning would have come with an ultimatum, and the likely nature of that ultimatum was scaring me witless. I certainly wasn't convinced by Eleanor's belief that Skaill wouldn't do away with Tim while he still owed him money.

On top of that, I was nagged by guilt. Last night I'd left Tim to his fate when both of us knew the black Mercedes parked near Bianca's had to be Skaill's men sitting generating testosterone. Now I was fastening my seat belt on a cosy Monarch flight to Manchester, leaving Tim badly injured in hospital, and Sian and Eleanor in danger.

\* \* \*

After Mike Haggard's late-night phone call, Eleanor and I had sat sipping our drinks, tossing wild theories back and forth about Tim's known troubles, and generally humming and hahing and getting absolutely nowhere except pleasantly tipsy. Which was good, as far as I was concerned. Eleanor's hearing wasn't sharp enough to have caught Haggard's words and, as she'd missed his reference to a leather jacket and almost everything else, I was content to let the talk move away from our problems with Ronnie Skaill.

When I left the bungalow, in the early hours of the morning, Eleanor kissed my cheek and reminded me to talk to Sian and insist that she move in with her and Reg. The door closed, I'd smiled ruefully as she walked away without locking it, and I knew that before I was in the car she'd have swapped her gin and tonic for ovaltine and would be sitting snug in bed alongside Reg, her diplomatic dipstick.

Dipstick or not, as I drove down from the upper Rock, I was pretty sure I would need all his diplomatic skills when putting Eleanor's proposition to Sian.

And so it proved.

'The plan is this,' I said. 'You drive me to the airport. Then you throw whatever you need into a holdall and move in with Eleanor.'

'Why?'

'A precaution. Better safe than sorry. A stitch in time. Things like that.'

'Ronnie Skaill doesn't bother me. I told you when you took that brother of yours down to the marina,' she said. 'I can look after myself, Jack. Surely you've known me long enough now to understand that without being told.'

She was sitting up in bed, slick with perfumed cream, I could smell the cool night air on my clothes as I sat as close to her as I dared. In the warm light from the bedside lamp she was the picture of soft femininity, her shining blonde hair tied up in some sort of white muslin, the lemon-yellow T-shirt that served as a nightdress stretched taut over . . . well, her well developed pectorals. The softness didn't quite reach her blue eyes. They were at once icy, yet flashing fire.

'Nobody better than you,' I admitted, 'when the situation is one you can control.'

'What, and this isn't?'

'Far from it. I've known you to teach young executives survival techniques in locations as bleak as Cape Wrath — but that was you against the elements, there were no enemies out to kill you. OK, I've also heard tales of your exploits in the Middle East deserts that would make lesser men than me quake in their DMS boots. But in all of those situations I've pictured you in a location that's been reasonably secure. You've been fully in control, dressed in the right gear and carrying weapons capable of knocking over an elephant. And you've had backup. You were not alone.'

'I'm not alone now,' she said, and smiled sweetly.

'But you will be when I'm in the UK.' I paused, let that sink in, then said, 'Take a look at yourself, Sian. It's night-time, and this could be tomorrow night — '

'Tonight. It's two in the morning.'

'Yes, all right, but here you are, unarmed, practically unclothed. Now turn the clock on a couple of hours and imagine yourself snoring — '

'It would have to be some vivid imagination. I do not snore.'

'All right, you're smiling sweetly as you dream of a dashing private investigator — '

'Hah!'

' — and then your dream is shattered as the patio doors explode inwards and Skaill's men — who've scaled the balcony — burst into this room and . . . well, need I go on?'

'Mm, you do go on a bit, don't you? You remind me of an old gramophone with a horn and a cracked record that — '

'I forgot to mention,' I said. 'This is not about you.'

'Damn,' she said, the ghost of a smile flickering in her eyes, 'now he's going to be crafty. He's got a hole card, and I think I know what it is.'

'When God made Reg he made an office boy not a bodyguard. I want you to be there to look after Eleanor.'

'Well, goodness me, why on earth didn't you say so?'

'Does it make that much difference?'

'Of course. Instead of a wimp sheltering behind a couple of oldies, I'll be a bodyguard. My considerable fighting qualities are not being impugned.'

I grinned. 'I'll be away a couple of days at the most. And without any intention of . . . what was that word?'

'Impugn.'

'Right, so without any intention of impugning those fighting qualities, I'll phone regularly to check that you and Eleanor are safe. All right?'

'And Reg.'

'Well, yes, of course. So, you'll do it. You'll stay with them?'

'For a dashing private investigator,' she said, lying back on the pillow with a smooth but deceptively strong forearm draped languidly across her brow, 'there's not much I won't do. Now, with that in mind, are you going to sit there for what's left of the night — or are you coming to bed?'

★　★　★

Now, airborne, with Spain a dun and undulating landscape 30,000 feet beneath the wings with the occasional snow-capped mountain peak poking through thin skeins of white condensation, I had something like three hours for reflection. I knew whatever thinking I did would begin and probably end with Sian Laidlaw, and with that I was content. Over several years and a number of crises, none worse than her horrendous accident on the Isle of Mull during the Bridie Button case[1], my Soldier Blue had become part of my life.

Long before that my own adult life had been crystallized by one incident in the Middle East, and some years later by a meeting with a unique Scot with a similar background to my own who had literally saved me from homelessness and the gutter.

During twelve years in the army, special investigation work had been just one part of a career that had seen action with a Royal Engineers parachute squadron and the SAS and ended abruptly and unexpectedly. In a rapid in-and-out action in Beirut I had killed an innocent man with my bare hands and his sightless eyes and the black blood seeping from his ears — the only sign of violence — had for the next twelve months gone with me each night to my bed. At the end of that

---

[1] *An Evil Reflection*

time, worn ragged from lack of sleep, I had reached a conclusion, and a decision.

The conclusion was that violence was not my way of life.

At thirty, jauntily whistling, the decision had taken me away from my army career and I'd spent the years until thirty-five wandering aimlessly downhill in a hot climate. I'd painted fences in the Australian outback and conducted coach loads of slant-eyed tourists around Alice Springs, and Uluru when it was still called Ayers Rock, but when I tried selling accident insurance on the streets of Sydney and cash registers in Brisbane the fists that had persuaded a commanding officer that the army and I should part company were of little use in coaxing laconic Aussie prospects to part with their cash.

When England beckoned I returned, penniless, and that first rain-swept night on the glistening streets of Brixton I strolled into a spit-and-sawdust pub and saved a man called Calum Wick from a savage beating by three huge Yardies who — as he put it — were desirous of making a wee profit from his wheeling and dealing. A short while later, as we laughed between groans and our blood stained the cracked basin in an evil-smelling public toilet, he told me about the profitable scam with amusement lurking in his deep-set

54

black eyes, for the twist in the tail was that the dealing that led to the fracas really was all about wheels: Calum, a man without a driving licence and, he told me, short of a driver, ferried stolen Mercedes saloons from Germany to Liverpool for a bent detective sergeant whose contacts had no scruples but very fat wallets.

Liverpool was my home and I saw well-paid, periodic trips north behind the wheel of a luxury saloon as an opportunity to visit old haunts and renew acquaintances, and for a time it worked well. But while my bank account went from red to black without hindrance from the Chancellor, the conscience that had once driven me from the SAS began pushing me with increasing frequency to the American Bar on Lime Street and a dark, alcoholic brooding. Alerted by the ex-boxer who was about to become owner, Calum whispered in my ear that the scam had run its course then led me next door to the first-floor offices of a private investigator called Manny Yates who was looking for an assistant with experience. That could have meant anything, but it led to a reasonably rewarding five years followed by a gradual drift away from those brown-linoleumed offices into military modelling and a skill I had not known I possessed, the beginnings of an uneasy contentment that lulled me without ever hiding the fact that something, still, was missing.

The muted drone of the Airbus was soporific. I yawned, stretched, glanced at my watch. Ninety minutes to go. I looked with sympathy and admiration at the two impressively cool flight attendant's making light work of dishing out refreshments in the cramped central aisle, then with more interest when I realized that one of the efficient young women was being given a hard time.

A young man sitting in an aisle seat was chatting her up. He was three rows in front of me, on the opposite side. The bright sun blazing through the window was putting his profile in sharp relief, and in light reflecting from the plane's curved ceiling I could see slicked-back dark hair, the tanned planes of a bony face and a familiar prominent nose. My pulse lurched; my scalp prickled. I was looking at Ronnie Skaill's eldest son, Terry, and I do not believe in coincidence.

Why was Terry Skaill making the trip to the UK? Or, more to the point, why was a man who lived with his glamorous blonde wife in southern Spain making the trip to the UK from *Gibraltar*?

He had to be following me, and it didn't take a genius to understand why. My short statement in the witness-box at a forthcoming trial would put his brother in prison for life, and there could be no better way of keeping me out of a Gibraltar courtroom than by bopping me on the head and dumping me in a dark alley a thousand miles away from the Rock.

Raised voices snapped me out of my disturbing reverie, and as I glanced at the unfolding scene I guessed Terry Skaill had overstepped the mark. There was a sudden concerted gasp from nearby passengers as the young woman being pestered leant across the trolley and smacked Terry backhand across his bony cheek. With a sharp crack, knuckles connected with cheekbones. Terry turned sideways, rolling with the young woman's full-blooded blow. As he did so, our eyes met and held. And, as the young woman straightened up, conversation resumed and the clinking trolley trundled to the next row, he grinned, winked at me, and drew a forefinger across his throat.

Heart thudding, I sat back again and shut my eyes.

So now I knew. But I'd known anyway — hadn't I? And anyway, what difference did it make? Gibraltar or Liverpool, I would constantly be looking over my shoulder for the next six months, or however long it took the Nick Skaill case to get to court — or for the Skaills to get to *me*.

The thought of violence hovering like a judge with a black cap, not just over me but over those I loved, brought me back, neatly, to Sian Laidlaw.

I had met her in Norway, she taking a break from military duty — instructing an intelligence cell on deep water exercises in high-speed inflatables — me on holiday and stepping gingerly onto skis for the first time since my own stint in uniform. Over many pleasant evenings seated before a roaring fire in the ski lodge I learned that this young woman who looked as warm and soft as honey and melted butter had seen her Scottish seafaring father lost overboard in an Arctic gale when she'd been ten years old and illegally aboard his ship, had returned to nurse her dying mother in the Cardiff slums and, years later, with a university degree under her Shotokan karate black belt, move north to become something of a legend among the high peaks of the Cairngorms. From there the army had seemed the most natural next step on her climb to the top.

Some time before the holiday that had brought us together I had bought Bryn Aur — the hill of gold — a stone farmhouse set against the foothills of Glyder Fawr and

Glyder Fach in North Wales. Across the yard from the main house, set beyond a massive oak tree, there is a workshop where I produce high quality military miniatures. It was there that I took Sian Laidlaw at the end of the skiing holiday (the house, not the workshop), and over the years since then my blonde Soldier Blue has shared my home and frequently my bed. But on more than one occasion I have caught myself reflecting that nothing's settled until it's settled, and the move to Gibraltar — mutually agreed — was proving to be yet another thorn, another fly in the ointment, another twist in a relationship in which the plot is always thickening.

Sian loved the heat, the white buildings, the glitter of sun on water, the exotic spicy scents that constantly reminded her that she was almost as close to Africa as Europe. I missed the thick stone walls of Bryn Aur and the stairs where my red-coated toy soldiers stood guard in shaded niches, the cold snows of North Wales and, yes, the back streets of Liverpool.

Was the move to Gibraltar a mistake?

I asked myself the question, but I'd left it too late. The pilot had started the descent into Manchester Airport, and I reluctantly fastened my seat belt and cleared my mind to make room for the bad news I knew would soon be delivered by DI Mike Haggard.

# 5

It was late afternoon when I took the Volkswagen Golf 1.6 S rented from Hertz into the sweeping right-hand curve at the eastern end of Llyn Ogwen's still waters and minutes later saw, away to my left and down across steep slopes of wiry grass and the rocky course of the tumbling Afon Ogwen, the stark stone buildings of Bryn Aur. Even from that distance — for I still had some way to drive down the A5 before I could make the sharp turn off the main road and double back along the river to my home — I could see light from the main window filtering through the leafy boughs of the big oak tree in the yard. Incongruously, too, there was a black car standing in front of the house when I clearly remembered parking my Audi Quattro at the back — and that was silver.

Interesting. I knew Calum Wick didn't possess a driving licence, and I'd assumed ageing scally Stan Jones would have driven him to Wales in his rusty white van. Dropped him and left at once, or perhaps remained with him to share drinks and yarns through the long evenings — but even if he'd done that, and from whatever distance, rusty white couldn't be mistaken for glossy black.

Then, when I'd left the main road and a mile or more of rough track had crunched and popped away beneath the tyres and I drove across the stone bridge over the river and up the short slope to the house, the interesting vehicle became intriguing and just a little bit creepy because I found myself pulling in alongside a gleaming Mercedes. Black. With tinted windows.

Thoughtfully, I climbed the couple of worn steps past the geraniums in their weathered stone pot standing amid yellowing dead leaves, clicked open the porch door and walked onto terracotta quarry tiles misted with condensation. There I kicked off my shoes, smiling wryly at the chill cutting through thin socks compared to the under-foot warmth I'd been used to on the shores of the Med, then pushed through the front door into the hall. At once the familiar smells of the house enveloped me, enfolded me and, as I passed beneath the staircase flanked by stone walls where proud toy soldiers stood guard in shadowy niches, I saw that Calum had remembered. The landing light was on, as it should be when anyone was in residence, the dimmer turned down so that the stairs seemed lit by pale moonlight. From my position looking up I could see in those niches reflections and highlights on glossy red coats, the gleam of silver paint on tiny muskets and swords, even the whites of watchful eyes.

My heart warmed to my old friend.

For he was there, all right. Along with the scents of stone and must and the dry cut pine logs I knew were piled in the wicker basket at the side of the inglenook fireplace there was one more that was the essential Calum Wick. Oh, white spirit and enamel paint were there too, of course, but those were smells that clung to both us and our surroundings, smells we carried around with us like a miasma or perhaps a cloak worn with pride. No, what I'd detected as soon as I'd pushed open the porch's outer door and stepped in from the cold was the rich aroma of Schimmelpenninck cigars. Calum smoked nothing else, and when I walked into the huge slate-floored living room I saw familiar leather furniture and thick scattered rugs, packed bookcases, and a faint blue haze clinging like valley mist to the red-shaded wall lights. Calum, sprawled full length on the chesterfield with stockinged feet poking bonily from faded jeans, had one arm folded across his maroon sweat-shirt. A slim panatella cigar jutted from his salt-and pepper beard and, through paint-smeared John Lennon glasses, he was reading a book on military uniforms.

'Just in time,' I said, slipping from my jacket and twirling it onto a chair like a swashbuckler's cape. 'Come on, my man, who are you and what have you done with the family silver?'

'Very little,' Calum said, eyeing me over his glasses, 'because you've kept it well hidden. That goes for food, too — or perhaps, as in the case of the silverware, you've neglected to buy any. Luckily for you I'm weak from starvation, or I would have felled you like a tree before you'd stepped through the door. You realize it was me thought *you* were the burglar?'

'Yeah, I noticed the sudden, lithe movement as you sprang into action.'

'Unsheathed my sword and prepared to defend your property? Aye, I can just see that happening.' He cocked an eyebrow. 'What the hell are you doing here anyway? I thought you'd turned into one of those queer fellows, what are they, hedonists or lotus-eaters or some such variety?'

'That was cut short. I was summoned to the Admiral Street nest where swarms of pointy-headed bluebottles lay eggs that hatch into insignificant fleshy beings called detectives.'

'Amongst other choice and invariably apposite handles,' Calum said, grinning. 'So what did our friend Haggard want?'

'Follow me. I'll talk while I make coffee, you listen and look wise.'

I dropped the Hertz keys jingling on the coffee table and went through to the kitchen. At my touch on the switch the strip light flickered then burst into life. I glanced through to the office, saw the steady red LED on the answering machine and knew there were no messages — or, if there had been, Calum had dealt with them — then filled the kettle and spooned instant coffee into two mugs.

Calum had shuffled soundlessly after me on the beige socks he bought in packs from Marks & Sparks, wore until they were holed then threw away, and was straddling a chair at the pine table. He'd swept a flat bottle of brandy from a shelf and was holding it at the ready. As the kettle hissed and sang I leaned back against the sink and rapidly sketched in enough of my family's troubles for him to get the gist. I also filled him in on the talk with Haggard and Vine.

'That double murder in the Liverpool fairground. The girl was Amanda Skaill. Apparently Tim was seeing her. Both the victims were knifed, and a cheap Chinese

64

knife with Tim's fingerprints was found by the bodies. And a man was seen running away from the dodgems: tall, slim, dark hair, wearing a leather jacket.'

'Could have been Tim, could have been anybody.'

'Yes. But there's more. Tim was involved in a fight at his apartment. One of the men involved was Nick Skaill. A neighbour described Tim, what he was wearing: a leather jacket. And yesterday Tim was seen getting on a flight to Gibraltar, wearing — '

'A leather jacket.' Calum nodded.

'Oh, and Haggard casually informed me he's got a brother, he's a cop, and he's flying out to help the Gib police. The only reason I mention that is that he's apparently got conflicting views on those murders.'

'Conflicting how?'

'Haggard wouldn't say. Probably not toeing the police line. Which could be helpful.'

I'd given Calum plenty to think about, and he was lost in thought as I completed the coffee making. Well, *almost* completed. I was limited to pouring boiling water onto granules. Calum added the finishing touches with a generous splash from the flat bottle into each steaming mug, and yet another enticing aroma drifted up to enrich the air.

I joined him at the table.

He said, 'That's quite a story. Strange goings on at both ends of a thousand-mile divide. However, as I'm now the man officially in charge of toy soldier manufacturing and have no connection at all to Scott Laidlaw Security — '

'Explain the Mercedes.'

'It's a car, it's German, it's outside. What's to explain?'

'Who put it there?'

'I did.'

'I gave it a swift glance in passing. The light from the house was reflected in the polished wood of the dashboard, the lustre of leather seats. I'm no great shakes at recognizing various makes and models, but that one out there appears to be the latest, and brand new.'

'Aye, it was given a grudging thumbs up by one Jeremy Clarkson.'

'So where'd you get the cash?'

'I have this part-time job in a sweat shop painting wee toy soldiers — '

'The sweat shop's your own humble flat in Grassendale, and car and flat are at odds with each other, they're a mismatch, the poor man living in one can't be reconciled with the fellow driving a rich man's car — '

'Bollocks.'

'Meaning?'

'Christ, you know I've got money, make

even more elsewhere.'

'Away from the sweat shop.'

'Where I'm paid a pittance.'

'Really?'

'Hey now, come on, what the hell started this — ?'

I took a deep breath. 'OK. I know about this *elsewhere*. Have always known, because there was a time when I was involved. And, surprise surprise, that too involved Mercedes cars.'

'A dodgy enterprise, as I recall, which you entered whole-heartedly. So what're those old saws about stones and glass houses, pots and kettles?'

'Yes. I know. I'm trampling on sharp fragments, wiping soot from my hands, beginning to regret.' I grimaced. 'I suppose the truth is I'm hot under the collar because . . . well . . . because of a couple of things. For one, I'm away from home — and I didn't realize that was bothering me. Well, Sian and I have touched on it, but . . . Anyway, the other is the tale I've just related: in the last couple of days the crimes I've become embroiled in involve my family. Too close for comfort. Skin-pricklingly scary. So to arrive here, my mountain sanctuary, and find you involved in some bloody scam — '

'Jack, Jack,' Calum said softly. 'You've been

rubbing shoulders with the wrong people. Your thinking has become seriously warped. There is no scam, bloody or otherwise. Stan Jones and I — '

I rolled my eyes. 'Damn it, and you talk about *me* being involved with the wrong people?'

Calum sucked in a breath. 'Now I wonder what Stan would say to that bit of pure undi-fucking-luted disparagement?'

'Yes, all right.' I held up my hands. 'Taken back. It was wrong, I shouldn't have said it, Stan's the salt of the earth.'

'Well . . . ' Suddenly Calum was grinning. 'I don't think that can be said of any of us, but if I tell you that what wee Jones the Van and I are doing involves racecourses all over the world and horses running and a certain complicated mathematical system Stan worked out on a cigarette packet when taking a rest from reading *War and Peace* — would that be enough to get you down from that beast you're riding?'

'My high horse?' I shook my head. 'No. It makes me even more uneasy, not to mention disbelieving — but I suppose it'll have to do.'

Silence reigned. Tempers went off the boil, simmered, cooled.

After a while, I said, 'You've got a Merc, but you can't drive.'

68

'I've always been able to drive.' He plucked at his beard, gave me a level look behind which devilment lurked. 'As a matter of fact, I learnt on the dodgems at a very early age.'

'Is that an attempt to get me back on the investigative track?'

'As in fairground, crime scene, brother in the shit?' He shrugged. 'You'll get there eventually. I grant you it'll take a wee while, you being what you are.'

'Which is?'

'A Sassenach. What is it they say about Englishmen?'

'They need time. But wasn't that Eartha Kitt? And didn't she sing it, tongue in cheek?'

'Not a pretty picture.'

I sipped hot, coffee-flavoured brandy. 'Being able to drive,' I said, 'isn't quite the same as having a licence to drive.'

'Investigating crime,' Calum said, 'is not quite the same as having a licence to investigate said crimes.'

'What's that supposed to mean? You're driving without a licence but it's OK because that's the way I work as an amateur PI?'

'Stan's white van separated into its various rusting components and became a heap of scrap metal,' Calum said. 'You wanted me out here in this godforsaken wilderness — '

'Unspoilt mountain paradise — '

69

' — and I was forced to admit that I've possessed a full driving licence for absolutely donkey's years. The car outside is the expensive result.'

'Well bugger me,' I said.

His grin broadened. 'Isn't that another thing they say about Englishmen?'

'First Eartha Kitt, now Quentin Crisp.' I rolled my eyes. 'But is that so unusual when the man in front of me has been known to wear a skirt when shopping in Tesco's?'

At that the banter suddenly stalled, then petered out. I could sense Calum wondering if we'd both gone too far, but if he could truly have read my mind he would have known that I had been speaking off the cuff, flying on autopilot. I'd listened without hearing, answered with whatever came into those vacant holes in my head that were not frenziedly trying to find a plausible explanation for the incriminating evidence presented to me by Haggard and Vine. The obvious one was that Tim's knife had been stolen. But why take it, carefully preserve Tim's fingerprints, then use the knife for a double murder? Was it a deliberate attempt to frame Tim, or simply a killer cleverly covering his tracks by leaving a false trail with what came to hand? Or both? The old saying of two birds with one stone updated into three with one stolen knife?

Eventually, of course, as the laced coffee was drunk and the mugs refilled and outside the kitchen window the weighty shadow of the big oak crept across the sloping yard that led down to my toy soldier workshops and the inevitable fine rain swept up the river, Calum came good by proving that if he couldn't read my mind he at least had the common sense to know where my thoughts lay.

And in true Calum Wick fashion, he hit me with a surprise that at once raised my spirits, gave me hope.

'You know,' he said, 'if what's been going on between us just now was actually serious stuff, there's a word for it in the dictionary.'

'Bickering? A domestic?'

'A *domestic*!' Calum said, throwing his head back in amazement. 'Man, will you listen to yourself, do you think we're man and bloody *wife* or something?'

'Go on then,' I said, grinning. 'What's this word?'

'Internecine. It means — '

'Yes, I know what it means. A struggle within. Governments do it. They fight amongst themselves, tear themselves apart.'

'As do criminal gangs.'

'Ah.' I thought about that for a moment,

couldn't see where it was leading. 'If you're referring to Ronnie Skaill and his various mobs, it would only make sense if Tommy Mack was a gang member. Someone wanted him out of the way so they could move up a rung, or they were making a point, putting the frighteners on somebody. But then the dead man would have to be a high up, wouldn't he? Otherwise his death wouldn't make waves.'

'You're looking at the wrong sex. One death that has certainly rocked the boat,' Calum said, 'is Amanda Skaill's.'

'God, yes,' I breathed. 'So where are you getting all this from?'

'Stan Jones. You know what he's like. He's a wee bald sponge with designer stubble, soaking up information from the Liverpool gutters.'

'And what he's picked up is that someone from within Skaill's organization killed the girl?'

'At first the merest whisper, swiftly developing into a rumour with substance.'

'And Tommy Mack, the dead man?'

'Collateral damage. He saw too much and had to go.'

'And talking of seeing, I wonder if the eye-witness saw more than he's admitting.'

Calum's eyes had narrowed.

'Someone witnessed the murders?'

'Not exactly. I told you, a man in a leather jacket was seen crossing the grass verge at the edge of the park.'

'The leather jacket link to Tim is too bloody flimsy — '

'Not if Tim got blood on it the way he told me he did. From Amanda, outside Jokers Wild. DNA will prove it's hers, and she's not there to back up Tim's story.' I flapped a hand helplessly. 'And then there's the knife, with his fingerprints.'

'And it was conveniently left at the crime scene. Come on! Even your brother cannot be that stupid.'

I smiled. 'Actually, I think he is, but I do know he's not a killer. I think it's obvious his knife was stolen, used, then left where it would be found by the police.'

Calum smothered a yawn by removing his glasses and stroking his beard.

'What a pathetic mess you two have got yourselves into. First there's you, opening your big mouth so that suddenly Nick Skaill's up for murder and looking at a life sentence that will happen over Ronnie Skaill's dead body.'

'*My* dead body.'

'Right, and then there's Tim, on top of his other troubles now suspected of murdering

73

Skaill's only daughter. When Skaill reads that in the papers there won't be a hole on the Rock deep enough for Timbo to hide in.'

'Right now he's hiding in hospital. Which I thought was reasonably safe, but is pretty exposed if the police are after him.'

'Or Skaill. It's about the worst place he could be. Skaill reads the news and there's Tim in bed in his PJs or one of those hospital gowns that leave most of your bum bare, muscles too damn stiff to move fast anyway, and his name's registered as an in-patient for all to see.' He shook his head. 'What about the others?'

'Sian's staying with Eleanor and Reg — which, reminds me, I told her I'd phone so it's time I called to check on all three of them.'

I left the kitchen table, slipped through into the office and sat at the desk. I glanced at my watch. Just after six. An hour later in Gib, but still early evening. I used the land line, and tried Eleanor's number first. It rang and rang. No answer.

Calum had wandered through and was leaning against the filing cabinet.

I tried Sian's mobile. Nothing. It went to voice mail. I left a message, asking her without any urgency in my voice to phone me when she got in.

Then I phoned our apartment in Castle Road. Nothing. Just the double purr of the ring tone, on and on, until I put down the phone and looked at Calum.

'Should I worry?'

'Of course. But not seriously, not yet.'

'Mm. They could have gone to a restaurant to eat — couldn't they?'

'Or maybe they're visiting young Tim in hospital.'

'I'm not sure Sian knows he's there.'

'She's an investigator. She *should* know. But as you can't reach her, why not try the hospital?'

I remembered on the plane asking Romero for the phone number, and stuffing the scrap of paper in my shirt pocket. I pulled it out, smoothed it on the desk, dialled the number. I got reception. Not knowing Tim's ward number meant there was a delay while the receptionist studied paperwork, made internal calls. When she came back on, the news was unexpected.

I put the phone down, screwed the paper into a ball, stared hollowly at Calum.

'He's not there. He *was* there, but he signed himself out. They don't know where he's gone, I don't know where he's gone, and I haven't got his mobile number. So now that's four of them I can't reach.'

'And you're thinking that the bad boys have begun applying pressure?'

'They certainly sent someone along to watch me. Terry Skaill was on the plane, and he made damn sure I saw him.'

'Stan knows that mob. We discussed. Terry comes across as a good lad when compared to the bunch he runs with. Probably here as an upright guy putting a gloss of respectability onto businesses he's checking on for Ronnie.'

I thought about that, let the idea soak in and dilute my fears. But thoughtful Calum was on another, more disturbing, tack.

'A thought occurs,' he said. 'Putting Sian and Eleanor together in one place sounded like an immensely good idea, but that bungalow is extremely isolated — and how sure are you that this Reg character can be trusted?'

*　*　*

We had a latish supper of pepperoni pizza, mixed salad with cherry tomatoes, straw chips fried to a deep golden brown, extra olives on the side for Calum — I cannot bear the taste of them — and drank most of a bottle of crisp white wine I'd picked up on my way through Betws-y-Coed. Then, while

76

Calum washed the dishes, I used dry kindling and half a packet of firelighters to light the fire in the living room's dog grate and was soon sitting in front of a crackling blaze.

But not comfortably, because I knew I had committed a serious blunder: I had foolishly moved Sian from the relative safety of our apartment close to Gibraltar town, and put her with Eleanor who lived in an isolated bungalow on the slopes of the upper Rock.

So I wasn't dwelling too much on Calum's question about how much I *trusted* Reg. What I was wondering was whether the retired diplomat-cum-office boy would be able to protect the two women if Ronnie Skaill decided to launch an assault.

Probably not a lot beyond token resistance which would swiftly lead to capitulation I decided ruefully, and I was gazing unseeingly but with considerable despair into the fire when Calum came through.

They say that when the mind is troubled, relief and solace can be found in work. And so it was that when Calum Wick walked into the living room carrying — and this really is true — two mugs of steaming cocoa and a plate of Scottish shortbread fingers — I at once launched into what amounted to a business meeting on the state of the toy soldier business known as Magna Carta.

We crunched biscuits and sipped our nightcaps and basked in the sultry heat of the glowing log fire that was bringing out the rich aroma of the leather seating as Calum reeled off the names of the sets he had completed and shipped and those that were either cast and waiting for painting, or painted and ready to be packed in their distinctive red boxes.

Highlanders, he said. Ten sets of Black Watch grenadiers, bandsmen, circa 1775. They were destined for New York, but there was no hurry. If instead I wanted him to drive in to Liverpool, link up with Stan the middle-aged Scouse scally and look into the double murder for which Tim was being hunted, then all I had to do was say the word.

So I did.

# 6

## Wednesday

Calum had been sleeping in the spare bedroom, and I knew the lanky Scot was always an early riser. But with unanswered telephones on the Rock making what sleep I did get fitful and so a waste of time, I was downstairs first and had prepared breakfast by the time he stirred. Several cups of strong black coffee washed down thick slices of toast and Oxford marmalade, then Calum yawned his way across the tree-shrouded yard draped in river mist to check that everything was switched off and secure in the workshop.

I went through to the office to telephone Luis Romero.

The Gibraltar detective inspector listened sympathetically to my story of the phone calls I had made, and how they had all gone unanswered. Orders snapped at subordinates while he was holding the phone demonstrated his authority for my benefit, and enabled him to tell me within minutes that neither Sian, Eleanor nor Reg the diplomat had been rushed into hospital with knife or gunshot wounds or indeed with the merest accidental scratch.

After some persuading he agreed to dispatch a police car to the upper Rock to check on Eleanor's house, and call me back. I put the phone down, passed the time by flicking through the file containing orders from toy-soldier retailers and wholesalers in the USA, saw that Calum had been correct and the retailer in New York was in no hurry for the Highland bandsmen because his next trade show was some months away, then jumped and sent orders and invoices spilling to the floor when the phone rang shrilly and nearly stopped my heart.

There was, Romero said, no sign of life at Eleanor's house. Then, just to reassure me, he said, 'Also, my friend, there is no sign of death.'

'What?' I said, heart still thumping, 'no crones in black frocks, no painted red cross on the door, no vultures circling?'

'Come on, Jack, you are worrying over nothing. Probably like your brother, they have crossed the border for some relaxation — '

'Hang on a minute, are you saying Tim's in Spain?'

There was a moment's silence on the line. Then Romero cleared his throat.

'Better we should talk face to face,' he said.

'When are you returning to Gibraltar?'

This sounded ominously like the response I'd got when in Eleanor's house talking on the phone to Mike Haggard. In his hardly subtle way, Haggard had been preparing me for bad news, and I couldn't see Luis Romero going all coy if his news was good. Grimacing at the thought of what might be waiting for me, I told Romero my plans and arranged to meet him later that day in his favourite Main Street bar.

He was still chuckling at his attempt at black humour when he rang off.

\* \* \*

Calum was out to prove that despite years away from the driving seat he was more than a match for my skills, his new German toy far superior to the impressive Hertz Volkswagen Golf. With the latter I wasn't about to argue. The trouble was that the smaller Hertz car's understandable inferiority prevented me from proving him wrong about the former. Or maybe not; a poorer driver than I would have been left for dead as we drove through North Wales, whereas I hung onto that crazy Scot in his black Merc like an insignificant weight being flung about at the end of a very weak elastic band.

81

We proceeded in that manner through country lanes, villages, small towns and so on to the motorways, until on the M56 when passing the Stanlow oil refinery I looked ahead and realized that Calum had been out of sight for some time and had undoubtedly taken the Runcorn exit which put him on the last lap of his drive to Liverpool.

Forcing my hands to relax — they had been trying to choke the steering wheel — I slowed to the motorway speed limit.

Thirty minutes later I was pulling into Manchester airport.

Five hours after that the Monarch flight had set me safely down on Gibraltar's tongue of a runway, a taxi had taken me to Casemates Square, and I was walking up a crowded Main Street towards the Copacabana. But not without several glances over my shoulder.

I had that uncomfortable tingling at the nape of my neck that invariably warns me I'm being watched, followed, or both. It had started in Manchester, saw me reaching up to massage the irritating spot several times during the three-hour flight, and showed no signs of going away. Usually it's not knowing who's giving my subconscious the willies that racks up the tension, but this time it was different and so I wasn't worried, just annoyed. I *knew* who was causing it. It was Terry Skaill. Just as on the trip to the UK, Nick Skaill's brother had accompanied me on the return flight and, whenever I turned around, it was to be met with a grin, a wink, or the hand raised with forefinger pointed and thumb crooked as if a pistol were being fired at my head.

★ ★ ★

The Copacabana bar and restaurant is located almost directly opposite Library Road. Romero was sitting at an outside table under one of those wide sloping sun canopies that crank out from a building's wall. He had a cappuccino in front of him and was opening a transparent packet containing the usual dry biscuit. From his position he had a clear view up Library Road to Library Square. As I approached he appeared to be tearing paper abstractedly while lost in contemplation of the trees that shaded most of that open space. Bathed in bright sunlight for most of the day, they created a cool oasis in the centre of the town and provided a rich green outlook for residents of the Elliott Hotel.

'I believe they have rooms in there, those two,' Romero said, nodding in the direction of the hotel as a way of acknowledging my presence. As I scraped back one of the metal chairs and sat down across from him, he turned his head and fixed me with his dark eyes. 'Do you know who I mean?'

Dark, suntanned, slim and dapper, pint-sized Romero was the antithesis of the scruffy working copper Mike Haggard liked to portray in his Admiral Street lair. The Gibraltarian police inspector wore expensive suits or casual clothes, always by Giorgio Armani, and knowing their prices I often speculated on the work he did during the moonlight hours.

'Becks and Posh Spice?' I ventured. 'Tony and Cherie, or perhaps Roger Moore — but doesn't the Saint favour the Rock Hotel?'

Seconds into the meeting I was already getting edgy. I was wasting time, sitting with Romero instead of rushing to the bungalow high up the Rock. The DI obviously saw something in my eyes that suggested tether's end being reached. He nodded, and made a soothing gesture with his expressive hands.

'I understand your impatience,' he said, 'but your brother's situation should also be of concern to you. I have already told you that he was observed by officials at the border being taken into Spain in the back seat of a Mercedes — '

'Whoa, now hold on a minute, you said no

such thing.' His words had hit me like a punch in the stomach. I leaned forward, slammed both hands flat on the table so that he was forced to grab his coffee. 'When I telephoned, you said something about crossing into Spain. There was no mention of him being *taken* there. And, for Christ's sake, isn't it obvious that if he was in a Merc it has to be the same one that was parked near Bianca's on Monday, the night he was beaten up?'

'If a Mercedes was there at Marina Bay, Monday night, its presence was not reported. No witnesses have come forward, and the car was certainly not there when your brother was found.'

'Well, of course, it bloody wasn't — '

'Then if you knew about it, why did you not tell us?'

'I . . . Look, let's come back to that. Go on, Luis, you were saying.'

'One reason your brother was noticed by officials was that he has extensive bruising to the face, an impressive black eye.' Romcro smiled coldly. 'But, still, it was not the facial damage on its own that attracted the officials' attention.'

'I bet it wasn't. The black Mercedes says it all. Tim wasn't going for a ride in the country with Becks and Posh, it was with two men. Probably pumped up with steroids, muscles straining the seams of expensive jackets, certainly wearing wrap-around shades. And I'll bet one of them was in the back seat with Tim, making damn sure he didn't communicate in any way with those officials who were standing there admiring his bruises while my brother was being kidnapped.'

'Even if the two men with your brother appeared to be . . . shall we say of a certain type? . . . the circumstances were not suspicious. All three men in the car appeared relaxed. Documents were in order, there was nothing the officials could do to hold the vehicle. Indeed,' Romero said, 'the idea of preventing those men from crossing the border did not occur to them. It was only later, when your brother's injuries were being discussed with some amusement and an alert official remembered the assault at Marina Bay, that my department was informed.'

'Not only later, but *too* late,' I said bitterly. 'They were Skaill's men, of course. But where the hell have they taken him — and why?'

'Those men,' Romero said, 'have nothing to do with Ronnie Skaill.'

'Tim owes Skaill money — '

'For the boat which some time ago your brother used in one or two abortive attempts to involve himself in a Skaill smuggling ring?' Romero nodded. 'Yes, I know that. But it is those men, with their flash suits and sun-glasses, who are staying at the O'Callaghan Elliott Hotel.'

'So what? Staying in a luxury hotel doesn't mean they're not a couple of Skaill's hard men.'

Patiently, Romero said, 'Give me some credit, Jack. We have been watching Ronnie Skaill for many years, and we liaise closely with the police across the border. This combined intelligence means that we are pretty sure we know all of the men who work for him. Their photographs are on file, and we know their names. These two are called John Raven and Pete Pagetti — those are the names they gave to the hotel, and their credit cards matched.'

'That means nothing at all. Credit cards come in cornflake packets. From the right people you buy one, get one free.'

Romero smiled wearily. 'Let's assume they're legitimate. So, if, as you insist, these two men who roughed up your brother and have now spirited him away across the border are work-ing for Skaill, then they are new recruits. But I do not think so. Here, in my gut' — he patted his flat belly — 'I think what is going on with these men and your brother is separate from Mr Skaill's activities. And that bothers me, because it is an imponderable — and on my patch I do not like imponderables.'

'Over the border,' I pointed out, 'is not on your patch. Once they'd crossed, there wasn't much you could do for Tim.'

He shrugged, neither admitting nor denying. He was still observing me closely. Perhaps he had recognized in my eyes the decision I didn't know I was about to make, the bombshell I hadn't dreamed I would drop.

'I've been thinking hard,' I said, slowly, and with reluctance. 'I've realized that if it comes to choosing between the safety of those I love, or putting Nick Skaill behind bars, it's a no-brainer, isn't it?'

But something, or somebody, had caught Romero's eye.

'Talk of the devil,' he said softly.

When I followed the direction of his gaze, I saw Nick Skaill. He was on the opposite side of the street. The stocky man walking with him wore a dark, pin-striped suit and was carrying a leather briefcase. His shiny black hair was receding, and rimless glasses rested on a prominent fleshy nose that jutted from a face bearing the sheen of money. Or perhaps he'd overdone the moisturiser.

They were walking fast but having to dodge dawdling pedestrians. Skaill dropped behind the other man as they passed by, and he spotted me, looked across and grinned. Like his brother he was tall and lean, with long untidy hair, a gaunt face and intense, deep-set eyes; suitably dressed, he would have slotted neatly into the cast of *Les Misérables*, but today he wore a loose black T-shirt, jeans and trainers.

'I thought you'd arrested him.'

'For a while after the nightclub killing he was away from the Rock. He had driven to his father's villa in Spain that night. It was his birthday, I think there was a small celebration. From Marbella he flew to the UK. He was back here two days later, the same journey but in reverse: flight to Spain, pick up his car, drive to Gibraltar. It was then we arrested him. You know, you were awaiting my call.'

'So why is he out?'

'The man with him is Gomez, his defence lawyer. He is good at his job. He fought hard to get his client released on conditional bail.'

'Which means?'

'We must know where he is at all times. And there is a night-time curfew.'

I was watching Skaill absently. They threaded their way through the crowds, moved out of sight. When I turned to Romero, he was looking at me intently.

'This thing you have realized. Before I

interrupted you. It is not difficult for me to work out, but if I am correct then I am appalled, rendered almost speechless.' His dark eyes had narrowed. 'Is that what you are telling me?' he said. 'You would retract your statement?'

'I've made no written statement.'

'No, that is true. But you came forward the morning after the death of an off-duty, senior police officer, Inspector Bobby Greenoak. There had been an argument, and he had been gunned down in cold blood. You didn't know that, but you told me that you were passing the Lagoon Deep nightclub down by the waterfront, and you heard a shot. You heard screams, a commotion. Then you heard footsteps, running, Nick Skaill burst from a side passage and raced away into the darkness. He had a gun in his hand. Yes? Isn't that what you said?'

'Mm. And I went in, saw the body.' I wagged my head from side to side, suggesting uncertainty. I could feel myself beginning to sweat. 'But the mind's a funny thing. It all seemed clear at the time, man running, a flash of metal in his hand when I'd heard a gun go off. I'm pretty sure it was Nick. But that metal . . . I don't know, the mind can play tricks. You hear something, see something, and suddenly they come together. A picture's created out of nothing. A false picture? Who knows. Thinking about it now, I realize Nick could have been carrying a beer can, or a mobile phone, the light glinted on whatever it was and — '

'Oh come on, Jack!'

'I'm thinking aloud, Luis. That's all. But I'm doing so because there's another picture in my mind, it concerns Sian and my mother — and it's not a pretty one. But — and there's always a but to boost flagging hopes, isn't there? — that too could be false. I hope it is. I hope there's a reasonable explanation for Sian and Eleanor not answering their phones. Because then everything would be back on track, I'd be waiting for my day in court, and this conversation never happened.'

'I sincerely hope it turns out that way,' Romero said, and suddenly there was a hard edge to his voice, a spark of anger in his eyes. 'Firstly because, naturally, I do not wish to see those women coming to harm, but secondly because if you take the course you have suggested then I too will then be left with no choice.'

I nodded. 'You'd be forced to subpoena me?'

'Exactly. It would be the only alternative. Even if I felt disinclined to take that course, my superiors would force my hand. So, yes, if you refuse to give evidence, Jack, a subpoena will be issued. And if you still refuse to testify, then you will almost certainly find yourself gazing at the sunlight through the bars of a cell in Moorish Castle.'

'A court appearance, or a cell. Spoilt for choice. But I may never experience either. I think I'm already being watched. Followed closely by those waiting for the right moment to squash me like an annoying fly.'

'Who? Who is watching you?'

'Terry Skaill was on the same plane as me, out and back. I felt menaced.'

'Unreasonably so.' Romero made a dismissive gesture. 'Skaill senior will be desperate. He is a parent with a burning desire to see his daughter's killer brought to justice. I think the Skaills know someone within the Merseyside police force, a civilian who is close to the action. This person, man or woman, is able and willing to pass on information for a small payment. I believe *that* is why Terry Skaill travelled to the UK.'

★ ★ ★

The thought of being incarcerated in Moorish Castle was decidedly scary. What's the saying, caught between a rock and a hard place?

We parted with that threat lurking in the background to haunt and unnerve me. Romero strolled inside the Copacabana. I guessed he would have another coffee, this time with a strong additive to recover from the shock I'd delivered. Or perhaps just to wipe out the memory of a man silly enough to think he could buck the system.

I watched him go, then made my way to the taxi rank in Cathedral Square. There are no distances to speak of in Gibraltar; the round the Rock road race is completed in under thirty-five minutes by average athletes. The taxi I hired took me out of the town via Ragged Staff and Prince Edward Road and up past Moorish Castle — which was beginning to give me the shudders — to open sunlit slopes at a pace that would have allowed a Welsh tractor to take the chequered flag, yet still managed to deposit me outside Eleanor's bungalow in little more than five minutes.

I paid the driver, then stood at the side of the narrow road looking at the house as he drove away in a drift of diesel fumes. And it was quite strange, because you get a feeling don't you? You know, without knowing why, if a house is empty or occupied.

There was somebody at home.

I ran lightly up the wooden steps and,

when I banged open the front door, saw Sian and Eleanor gaping at me in shock I could have laughed out loud from pure relief.

Except I didn't.

A skinny man in a track suit, with grey hair tied back in a pony-tail and blue eyes as hot and dangerous as lasers, cast a fierce look in my direction then charged with his head down like an angry goat. He couldn't have weighed more than ten stone but his momentum made it feel like twenty and he sent me flying backwards. My body went out through the open door before my feet could move. I fell flat on my back, bumped my way painfully down the steps with the lean man riding me like a bob-sleigh on the Cresta. Then, as someone screamed shrilly, I found myself prostrate in the road with a bony forearm clamped across my throat and those terrifying blue eyes gazing into mine with murderous intent.

# 7

'I say, old boy,' Reg said, 'damn sorry about the brutal assault but I really did believe you were one of Skaill's thugs out to do serious damage to these precious young ladies.'

'Think nothing of it,' I said, feeling the words as a throbbing ache in my bruised throat.

'Actually,' he went on, 'I would have thought, being ex-army, you'd have instinctively called on unarmed combat techniques, flipped the silly old fool off your chest and shattered his larynx with a well-directed half fist to the throat.'

'*Ex*-army says it all,' Sian said, smiling sweetly at my discomfort. 'That's why he keeps a lanky ex-SAS Scottish bodyguard. And sticks close to me. Civilian life's turned him into a wimp.'

I was standing by the wash-basin in the bathroom. Sian had bathed the elbow I'd grazed when I slid down the steps into the road with Reg on top of me, and was finishing off with strong antiseptic before putting sticking plaster on the goriest red bit. Reg Fitz-Norton, wiry frame relaxed in his track suit, was leaning in the doorway watching.

As I tried in my manly way to suppress a series of winces, I could hear Eleanor in the kitchen doing something noisy with crockery. For the first time in my life I'd seen her visibly shaken. Hers was the shrill scream that had accompanied my slither down the steps; hers were the earlier instructions that I assumed were responsible for unleashing killer Reg. She'd told me before I was ushered into the makeshift A & E that when sitting in bed discussing tactics she'd quoted my favourite maxim to him: if Skaill bursts in here, him or any of his thugs, get in first, get in fast, get in hard — and this afternoon she had watched in horror as Reg followed her instructions to the letter and leaped on her son like an out of control pit bull.

Way over the top? More behind his explosive actions than a whispered list of tactical does and don'ts from Eleanor? I absently watched Sian, busy fingers efficiently ministering, and remembered Calum's question. Could I trust this man? Had this incident put any kind of trust in serious doubt? Or had he, valiantly, heroically, been doing the best an ageing diplomat could for the safety of the ladies in his care?

'Can I say something?' I said mildly.

Reg looked apprehensive.

Sian said, 'As long as it's not another 'Ow'.'

'Far from being a wimp,' I said, 'I deliberately held back when I was attacked because hitting an elderly, retired person would have been a cowardly — '

Whatever else I was about to say was drowned by the chorus of hoots and jeers that echoed from the bathroom's white tiles. Holding my hands up in surrender, I followed Sian and Reg into the living room where Eleanor was waiting with coffee and a fruity cake-type thing she bakes which I think is called a tea loaf. There was a knife and unsalted butter there, too, for those who believe the richer the cake the more help it needs to slide down.

'So, who's going to go first?' I said, when we were all settled comfortably with cups and plates balanced and the sound of knives spreading and spoons stirring had died away. 'Is someone going to tell me where you three vanished to, or would you like to hear how my brother Tim is being hunted by police across Europe for a double murder?'

Eleanor's knuckles went to her mouth. She looked wildly around the room, as if seeking solace in normality, then shook her head.

'Oh God,' she said. 'Oh dear God. Here was me thinking things couldn't get worse than Ronnie Skaill going after him for all that money. So what are you sayin', Jack? I thought that blood on his jacket was the Skaill girl's?'

'It's hers all right, and it got there when Tim used his own knife to murder her and a bloke called Tommy Mack in a Liverpool fairground. According to Mike Haggard, that is.'

I was puzzled. The look on their faces told me the news came as a complete shock to them.

'Haven't any of you read the papers?'

Eleanor shook her head. 'Reg doesn't bother with them. He goes on line, and then only looks at the financial stuff.'

'Well, it's all there, apparently. I argued with Mike Haggard, warned him he hadn't got enough to go public, but I can understand his confidence. Amanda Skaill and Tommy Mack murdered. The knife was left at the crime scene. Tim's fingerprints are on it. And someone very like him was seen running away.'

'Good news and bad news,' Sian said flatly. 'The knife's damning, the supposed identification not worth a toss.' She frowned. 'Where is Tim, anyway? You left him on the canoe. If he stayed there, surely he'll have been arrested by now.'

'If only it were that simple,' I said.

As concisely as I could I filled them in on all that had happened since Sian drove me to the airport. Clearly television news was avoided as much as the newspapers, for everything I told them came as a shock that for a while left them speechless.

Reg had moved over to sit on the arm of Eleanor's chair. One hand was lost in her silver hair as he gently massaged the nape of her neck. She had her eyes closed and, hand pressed to her breast like an American at the playing of the Stars and Stripes, was making an effort to calm her breathing.

Reg looked towards the door. His lips were pursed as he thought through what I'd said.

'I know your brother owes that bastard Ronnie Skaill a lot of money' — he smiled apologetically and patted Eleanor's shoulder — 'but now, in addition to this double murder business, there seems to be something else he's up to that we don't know about. Is that correct?'

The question had been directed at me. I pulled a face.

'I don't know. I'm not sure *Tim*'s up to something else. Those two men in the Merc certainly are: Pagetti and Raven, according to Luis.'

'Let me rephrase that: he's *involved* in something else.'

'Well, yes. Unwillingly, I would say. You don't voluntarily jump into a car with men who've recently used brass knuckles and boots to put you in hospital.'

'You're right, of course.' Reg was nodding slowly. 'They softened him up, now they've taken him into Spain. Bit convoluted, isn't it? What's so special about your brother that they'd go to all this trouble?'

'Tim specializes in cocking things up,' Eleanor said. 'I wonder if they realize that.'

'His only link with Spain,' I said, 'is Ronnie Skaill. But Romero's positive those two men don't work for Skaill.'

'So think the opposite,' Reg said. 'If they're not *for* Skaill, they're against him.'

'As Eleanor just pointed out,' I said, 'Tim would make a piss poor hit man. But if that's what they want, and he's taken Dad's Verney-Carron shotgun with him, most of southern Spain'll be running for cover.'

'I don't think they want Skaill dead,' Reg said. 'If they did, they'd spend a few thousand euros hiring a beach bum crazy for his next fix. Point him in the right direction, job done, no comebacks.' He grimaced, and spread his hands. 'No, I'm afraid Tim has been selected for his special qualities.'

'Eleanor's already told you what they are,' Sian said.

And again there was silence as I looked across into Eleanor's tormented blue eyes and the two of us who knew Tim so well racked our brains and tried to come up with just one special quality that might have marked him out for selection.

'If it's not a hit, if he's not been taken over there to blow Ronnie Skaill into a thousand nasty bits with that shotgun,' Eleanor said at last, 'what the hell has he been selected for?'

'As we don't seem close to working that one out,' I said, 'how about this. Last night I was watching the Welsh rain drifting across my yard and having an impressive litter of kittens because phone calls to Reg's 'precious young ladies' had gone unanswered. Luis Romero, when I phoned him this morning, couldn't help — so where were you all?'

'I've got a house on Europa Road,' Reg said, 'quite near the governor's residence — didn't Eleanor ever mention that?'

'I believe she did. Weren't you staying with Reg a couple of years ago, Eleanor, when Sian and I were in Gib? We were at the Rock Hotel, on a flying visit during the Sam Bone case[1]?'

'I was,' Eleanor said. 'And that's where we've been while you were over there

---

[1] *A Bewilderment of Crooks*

listening to Mike Haggard's barefaced lies.'

She'd slipped away from Reg's soothing hand and crossed to the window, returning almost at once to stand with arms folded. Reminding her of my UK visit had been a mistake. It had brought all the worry of the double murder flooding back, and her mouth was set in a thin line as she shook her head in disbelief, or frustration.

'Eleanor,' I said, 'Mike was doing me a favour, telling me in confidence what the investigation has uncovered so far. He wasn't lying. He was warning me that the finger-prints on the knife were Tim's and — '

'I can't believe you were fooled. Because he's wrong. Anyway, whatever you want to call it, facts, fiction or an obvious bloody frame up, with you away Reg thought we'd be safer at his place than staying here.'

'Yes, and so much for my fearsome reputa-tion,' Sian said. 'I was guest and bodyguard, with an impressive CV, but that didn't deter dear Reg. He moved us out, thought solid stone walls and ornate wrought-iron bars over quite small windows would make us all feel safe until the intrepid warrior returned.' Her eyes crinkled as she looked at Reg. 'I must admit you had a point. I slept like a log instead of jerking awake every time a floor-board groaned or a mouse stretched and yawned and reached for the cheese.'

'Yes, well,' Reg said, grinning, 'now that all the cans of worms have been opened, the case of the unanswered phone calls has been solved and the intrepid warrior is back in town — I'm off.'

'Off?' Eleanor swung on him. 'You heard Sian, she was staying here for our mutual protection while Jack was away — and that was your protection as well, you skinny old bugger. Now he's returned she'll be going back to their place with him, so I need you more than ever.'

'Steady old girl, steady,' Reg said. He was also up on his feet, and was holding his hands up, palms out. 'Remember, I told you earlier I had to go out? I'll be gone for a couple of hours, my love, no more. All I'm going to do is check emails, answer any that are from London, and urgent. Goodness, I'll be back before you know it.'

'We'll wait,' I said, glancing at Sian for confirmation. 'Natter for a while, have supper with you.'

Sian nodded agreement. Reg flashed me a grateful look. He'd crossed to Eleanor while he was talking, and finished off by taking her shoulders in both his hands and kissing her tenderly on the forehead.

'So that's settled then,' he said.

'Yes, well, fair enough, but don't you ever 'steady old girl' me, Reg Fitz-blooming-Norton. And make sure you are back here in a couple of hours or the door's getting bolted in case that bastard does turn up.'

She punched him on the shoulder as he turned away, her face softening and a hint of moisture glistening in her eyes as tension gave way to a measure of relief. She watched him go. The door closed soundlessly behind him. We heard him tripping lightly down the steps and shortly afterwards a car started and drove away into the long straights and sweeping curves that would take him several hundred feet down the Rock to his house on Europa Road.

We'd already eaten, so my mention of supper had really been nothing more than something calming to insert into an argument that was becoming heated. Instead, we sat and did the nattering. I put flesh on the previously skimpy story of my lightning visit to the UK, went deeper into my talk with Haggard and Vine, then enjoyed watching Sian's eyes widen in disbelief when I told her that Calum Wick had a driving licence and was now the proud owner of a Mercedes Benz.

Mention of that car, of course, took us all uncomfortably back to young Timbo and the

Mercedes with tinted windows that had been parked near Bianca's on the night of his terrible beating. From there it was a short step to his being borne away to Spain in what appeared to be the same vehicle. As floorboards did indeed creak in the silence — drawing a fleeting smile from Sian, who yawned and mouthed 'cheese' — and we sat there, lost in grim thought, footsteps pounded on the steps, the door we had neglected to lock behind Reg banged open, and Ronnie Skaill and his merry men finally came storming in out of the night.

# 8

## Thursday

Skaill's two goons had come in first, whacking the front door so that it hit the wall and bounced then stepping through and to either side so that Skaill could make his entrance between them. It was pure ham. Think American gangster movie or war film and you'll have seen the same manoeuvre. Trouble is, that doesn't mean it's not effective to the point of petrifying when it happens in front of you, in real life.

When the mob burst in, nobody had moved. Eleanor was in her favourite chair, legs elegantly crossed, Sian on the *chaise-longue*, stretched out on the fringed blankets as she fiddled with her pony-tail and an elastic band. I'd been standing — I think we'd actually decided that Reg was being so long looking through his emails that a drink of some kind wasn't such a bad idea after all.

Once in, Skaill had begun striding the length of the room, from rugs to bare floor, bookcase to wall, swivel, back again. The only illumination in the room came from the red table lamp. And it's funny how perceptions change. With the arrival of Skaill and his hoodlums, light that had seemed soft, warm and romantic had become blood-red and sinister. It followed Skaill, so that in one direction he was chasing his shadow, in the other it chased him.

While he paced, he'd talked. His two pumped-up goons had stood there, a couple of wooden Indians, legs apart, hands folded in front of their groins like premiership footballers in a two-man wall. In contrast to their black suits, white shirts, steroidal bulk and wrap-around shades, Skaill could have been a breath of fresh air. He was a tall, bony figure, shoulders stooped, long, tanned face gaunt and deeply lined. He wore an immaculate white shirt with broad, pale blue stripes, soft, brushed denim trousers over a pair of those sandals that are good for a Seychelles beach or the long trek to Everest base camp. Sharp black eyes were set in deep craters under shaggy brows. His hair was white, brushing the shoulders of his loose, alpaca jacket, and from that and knowledge of his past life I guessed his age at something over sixty, probably less than seventy.

Only, a breath of fresh air is what Skaill was not. Never. He was dressed like someone enjoying a package holiday on a Greek island, but the image was ruined by crude blue tattoos covering most of both forearms, and heavy gold bracelets that clanked like manacles as he paced. And what he exuded was not wafts of perfumed sun block but waves of palpable menace. A lot of it came from eyes that would have made a dead cod's look warm and expressive. Most was locked in a body that seemed to be an explosion waiting to happen. It was as if he'd been moulded from Semtex 10, and at some indeterminate time in his past a slow-burning fuse had been lit.

Skaill was well aware of the effect he had on ordinary folk, and he'd always used it to his advantage when carving out his crooked mini-empire. For some reason he was adopting a different approach, and most of his talk had been about how he meant us no harm. How the shock entrance had been intended to have the impact of a stun grenade because he didn't know what he was walking into. How he was sorry if he and his men had frightened the ladies — this said with what he believed to be a disarming smile flashed in their direction. And all this transparent bullshit had taken something less than a couple of minutes: shock entrance, goons in position, Skaill doing his walking and talking — and then, as the disarming smile shattered against the stony faces of ladies who were not for turning, he'd stopped his pacing and snapped something in my direction.

'Sorry,' I said now, as politely as I could manage. 'I must have missed that.'

I was now sitting next to Sian, but couldn't remember how I'd got there without crushing her outstretched legs. Eleanor, seeing my confusion, filled the void.

'The man wants to know where Tim is, darling,' she said.

'I thought he knew.'

'Same here. Wasn't it those two pillocks there who took him?'

'Two very like them.'

'An' now it's me who's missin' something,' Skaill said in a pissed-off voice straight out of a grimy Toxteth back street. 'What the fuck are you two talkin' about?'

'Tim was beaten up,' I said. 'Then he was escorted from his hospital bed by two men. They crossed the border into Spain in a black Mercedes — like the one I'm sure you've got outside.'

Skaill rolled his eyes. 'So what? You think I came here on a bike? And I already know what *happened* to your brother, but you repeatin' it just tells me again where he was, not where he is.'

'So it wasn't your men?'

'Christ, no, we've been playing catch up. I had Lord Soft Lad tracked from boardin' the plane in Manchester, landin' here in Gib then spendin' time at your place before headin' for the boat. So much for fuckin' intelligence. Not much good when lines of communication are ignored, is it? I got to know too late every time, an' someone was always there before us.'

'You were preoccupied. While all that was going on, your son was being arrested and charged with murder.'

Skaill had stopped his pacing, and had perched on the edge of my favourite rocking chair. He looked at me hard and shook his head.

'Jesus, you're a case, you are,' he said. 'But, as it happens, you've inadvertently brought us to the nub. It being the notion that two random and totally unconnected events — one still to happen, or not, depending — can be discussed. By us. You and me. Tonight.'

'One of the benefits to emerge being,' I said, 'that son Nick walks.'

'As does your brother, who's soon to be accused of murderin' my daughter.'

'Which doesn't seem to have upset you.'

'She was like her ma. No fuckin' good. Now it looks like she'll be worth more to me

110

dead than alive. And that's sound, isn't it? A reason for rejoicin'.'

'All right,' I said, cautiously, 'so why don't we drink to that, then you can tell us in detail what you're on about?'

'Scotch on the rocks for me,' Skaill said. 'Four fingers.'

'Yeah, well, what you'll get from me is two raised fingers for your cheek,' Eleanor said, standing up quickly, the polished ornamental bones in her necklace clicking like worry beads. 'You think I'm taken in by all this?' She waved a hand, an all-encompassing gesture sweeping up Skaill and his two impassive hard men.

'All this is nothing,' Skaill said, 'to the shit that would have descended on you, darling, if I was in a really bad mood.'

'Which is exactly what I'm saying. He might be fooled' — another gesture, this time dismissive, in my direction — 'but he's acting as soft as his brother. You and this, 'I don't mean any harm, you're all safe with me, sorry if we scared you'. That's a load of crap, the words of a crafty con man oilin' the wheels, stacking the deck, preparing to deal off the bottom. Well, forget it. They're my sons; if you're doing any dealing you do it with me, and in the end it comes down to this . . .'

She stopped, took a deep breath. Her face

was flushed, but with anger not exertion. I'd never seen her so riled. Skaill had never seen her at all, unless he'd noticed her as an unknown but charming lady window-shopping on Main Street, and I could see he was caught on the horns of one of those dilemmas. Knock her down before she gets too uppity, or let her keep talking? His cold black eyes were unreadable. He was watching and listening, but his patience was wearing thin.

'It comes down to this,' Eleanor repeated when she'd recovered her poise. 'You've lost Tim, right, haven't got a clue where he is, so bang goes any hope of getting back the money he owes you. But Jack's still here, exactly where you want him. What you're going to do is threaten him: do this, do what I want, and you'll be OK. Otherwise . . . ' She shook her head. 'Otherwise — and we all know what that means. When Jack turns you down, tells you to go an' jump — as he will, because he may be soft but he's not bloody stupid — one of those big daft gawps standing over there will pull out a gun and it'll be all over.'

'So what do you suggest?' Skaill said softly.

'I'll relent. We'll have that drink. But it goes like this, Mr Big Time. While you're sorting out what you're going to say that can sound anything like convincing, tell those big lads to

112

bugger off back to the car. They can wait for you there. I've got a feeling it won't be too long.'

Skaill was leaning back, arms folded, rocking gently. He looked at me and raised an eyebrow. I shrugged. Eleanor walked over to the drinks cabinet. Sian winked at me and went into the kitchen for the ice. Skaill looked at the two goons.

'Georgia, Cazza, you heard the lady. Make yourself scarce, but not extinct.'

He jerked his head, and they left the house like shadows banished by a shift in the light. He caught my eye, and glowered.

I said, 'Talkative, aren't they?'

'If I wanted to talk people to death,' he said, 'I'd keep parrots.'

He was watching Eleanor the way a hen watches a fox. Whatever he'd been expecting, it wasn't somebody that feisty, and she'd knocked him off balance. I wondered if he'd been henpecked by one of his wives. Or all of them. I think he'd had three. The latest, I recalled, was the typical blonde bimbo, probably chosen because coming up with one intelligent word would be difficult, two impossible.

'So, let discussion commence, Ronnie,' I said when crystal glasses had been passed around and we'd tasted our drinks.

113

'Your clever ma's already spelt it out. And she doesn't think much of you, does she? I deal with her, or not at all. The bogey is, there's only one person in a position to deal, and that's you, Scott.'

'If you talk at all,' I pointed out, 'we're all going to hear it.'

'Right, so here it is. Never mind what you heard from DI Mike Haggard — and, yeah, I do know you've been there and you and him are muckers from way back. What he told you is wrong. Lord Soft Lad did not commit murder. He didn't stick a knife into my daughter. He didn't cut that feller's throat.'

'Glory be,' Eleanor said softly.

'And if you were really listenin' and not just flappin' your ears,' Skaill went on, 'you bein' a PI will have picked up something important in what I just said.'

'You know details that were not in any of the newspapers.'

'Exactly. Proof of the puddin'. How each of 'em was cut. How they died. I know what I'm talking about.'

Sian gripped my arm, swung her legs down and leaned forward, her eyes intent on Skaill.

'But there's only one possible deal, and we all know what it is,' she said. 'If Jack swears that he will retract his statement and refuse to stand up in court and testify against your son, you, Mr Skaill, will give us the name of the person who murdered your daughter.'

She flashed Eleanor a reassuring glance, then looked quickly at Skaill. The crooked ex-pat was up off the rocking chair, and walking. He reached the front door, opened it, and the cool night air tumbled in like a presage of doom.

'You're absolutely right,' he said, lingering. 'Yeah, that is the deal. So all we need is a yes or no from him over there.'

'What I need is time to think.'

'Christ, I must like you, because I'm going to be soft, stick my neck out, trust you. Within the next twenty-four hours I'll deliver the fairground killer to you. Then you've got a further twenty-four to keep your side of the deal.'

I frowned. 'Not just the name? You'll physically hand him over, in person?'

'Absolutely.'

'With proof of his guilt?'

Skaill shrugged. 'Of course. No point, otherwise. So there you are, grandiose gesture, best you've had all day.'

'Fanfare. Roll of drums,' Sian said. 'Fireworks over the bay.'

'Whatever, but I've said my piece.'

I shrugged. 'You say you're going to trust me, but can I trust you?'

'I couldn't give a shit. The bigger of my two lads, Georgia, he's a Yank from the state where they hold the Masters golf, used to be a military sniper. And if I haven't got the right answer twenty-four hours after the fairground killer gets dropped on your doorstep, some day between now and my boy's trial a slug from a C14 Timberwolf rifle is going to hit you right between the eyes.'

# 9

'Tim,' Calum Wick said, 'has probably been getting into hairy situations like this for most of the time he's been out of your sight — and that's years, isn't it?'

'More away from us than with us. Out of sight and certainly out of my mind, which makes seeing at close hand the mess he makes of his life even more of a shock. For Eleanor especially, because she's eternally optimistic.'

'Aye, but what was it they said about Bo Peep's sheep?'

'Leave them alone and they'll come home?' I was sure Calum could detect the sadness in my laugh. 'Well, that's all I can do, as I don't know where the hell he is. As for the rest, from the description of the men who took him — and knowing he's already had a taste of their viciousness — I'd say he'll have to pay dear for his freedom.'

'And so,' Calum said after a pause for reflection, 'we come to Ronnie Skaill's visit.'

'Got any ideas?'

'He was testing the water. There was no deal, on or off the table. Christ, he knows you're not going to back off. So he came visiting. Weighing up the opposition, if you like. And my guess is he found it wanting.'

'I think I detect an insult, a slur on my character.'

'Depends on what your terms of reference are. If you and those gals you have with you are found wanting when judged by Ronnie Skaill's standards, I'd say that's no bad thing.' He paused, came back thoughtfully. 'Reg the diplomat, however, is a different kettle of fish — wouldn't you say?'

'Mm. Absent from the fray. I wonder if that was deliberate. Did he know Skaill was on his way? And if he did, how? I'm beginning to share the mistrust you hinted at, but it still leaves me with a powerful rifle pointing at my head and knowing very little about just about anything.'

'Aye, well that's where we come in. The great Scottish detective and his wee Scouse sidekick.'

'Jones without a Van.'

'Not any more. The man's got one of those boxy Citroëns, looks like a van with windows. These fairground murders combined with his new mode of transport are giving him ideas above his station. He's taken to cruising the streets to see what it'd be like selling ice cream.'

'But also, I sense, cruising with a more serious purpose.'

'And considerable intelligent circumspection. On my part, that is. As Amanda Skaill was the scion of what we in the know call a rat pack of crims and low lifes, I thought it best to employ an outflanking manoeuvre. I talked to Tommy Mack's brother.'

'Which is all about helping Tim, but doesn't do much for me and that rifle.'

'Wheels within wheels. One thing invariably leads to another, and when we've got enough of those it's often possible to establish a connection which leads to a denouement.' He chuckled. 'My day for big words. Anyway, you'll no doubt be surprised to learn that what came out of the aforesaid conversation had nothing to do with Tim, or murder.'

I had picked up Eleanor's phone and called Calum almost as soon as Ronnie Skaill had clattered down the steps. I'd watched from the window. He'd been driven away in one of those black Mercs that for my liking look too much like hearses waiting for a body. Reg still hadn't returned. Eleanor had ruled out any mention of him with a dismissive flap of the hand, yawned, stretched, kissed me on the forehead and floated away to bed to dream about Tim's get-out-of-jail card. Sian was again stretched out on the *chaise-longue*. She

119

was wrapped snugly in the colourful Moroccan blanket Eleanor uses for afternoon naps, and was watching me from under eyelids that persisted in drooping towards sleep.

They both closed as I looked at her. Then one fluttered opened again.

'If he's in Liverpool or North Wales and he's got a land line where he is,' she said woozily, 'get him to call back. You're on his mobile, and it's Eleanor's phone bill.'

I gave her the thumbs up as she let that eye close and began to purr, discovered Calum was at his flat overlooking the Mersey in Grassendale, relayed Sian's message and he rang off. When he came back on, seconds later, I'd turned out the red-shaded light and was sitting with my sleeping Soldier Blue in a room bathed in limpid moonlight.

'Right, go on,' I said. 'You'd got as far as Tommy Mack's brother and me being surprised.'

'He's a young man name of Eddie,' Calum said, 'toting a veritable goody bag of extraordinary information which he was happy to spill on the table. I spoke to him in the Jolly Miller over a pint of John Smiths Extra Smooth. He was not so much upset at his brother's death as angry at the notoriety the murder had dumped on him. Media camped on his doorstep, constant harassment, you know the routine. And I can see his

120

point. If you're a quite ordinary fellow with a good job and a family it's not conducive to peace of mind when you discover your scallywag of a brother had close links with Ronnie Skaill's disreputable crew.'

'Did he now? Tommy? Well, it is a surprise, but the man's dead so how can it help us?'

'I'm not sure. It does open various channels that are worth investigating. For example, Tommy boasted to his brother that he was the other chap using fists and boots with Nick Skaill when Tim was set upon in his Albert Dock apartment.'

'Again, I can pass that on to Mike Haggard, for what it's worth, but I still can't see where this is going.'

'It seems that before things got nasty, the atmosphere in Tim's apartment was reasonably friendly. Drinks were shared before visitors became attackers, Tim the attacked. Or should that be attackee? The point is, in those convivial ten minutes or so, Nick was quite taken with Tim's display of original water-colours.'

'Didn't know he had any.'

'Indeed he has. Only two or three, as far as I could make out, but worth a lot of money. However, that could now be academic as far as Tim's concerned, because I'm not entirely sure what happened to them. Not sure, but

121

with a sneaking suspicion — you see, what interests me is that Nick brought his dad into the conversation. He told young Tim that Ronnie has an impressive art collection nailed to his stucco walls over there in Marbella.'

'Right. And that interests you because . . . ?'

'Aye, well, as I say it's just a wee thought that's niggling away at the back of my mind. We know Tim's in Spain. I've discovered that he had desirable water-colours. If they've disappeared, well, we know Nick Skaill was in Tim's apartment and if he plundered it that leads to the obvious conclusion.'

'Plundered?'

'You having trouble with that?'

'No, no.' I thought over what he'd said, and suddenly I had the same sneaking suspicion. 'So Tim's water-colours may by now be gracing Ronnie Skaill's walls. I suppose he could look on them as part payment for the money owing on the canoe, though he's not going to tell Tim that. But it still doesn't explain what those two blokes are doing. Why hammer Tim badly enough with boots and brass knuckles to put him in hospital, then get him to sign himself out so they can take him across the border?'

'I know. I can see Tim hiring a couple of thugs to get his paintings back. But if we *are* heading in the right direction then it's as if they beat him up to force him to recover his own paintings.'

'The only possible explanation is that they tracked those paintings from Tim's apartment to Skaill's villa, and want them for themselves. And that throws a different light on Eddie Mack. If those thugs know about Tim's water-colours, he must have passed the information to them, and that rather spoils the image of a contented family man with a decent job.'

'I don't think so. My gut feeling is that Eddie Mack's genuine. I'm not sure on the precise chronology of events, but I think you'll find Tommy Mack had time to pass on the information before he strolled into the park to meet Amanda Skaill and ended up getting his throat sliced.' He paused. 'A possible reason for which, incidentally, Eddie Mack hinted at in a parting shot.'

'When you'd both quaffed your John Smiths Extra Smooth.'

'Quaffed?'

'Mm. You having trouble with that?'

Calum snorted. 'What Eddie told me was that Amanda had done something so bad it was eating away at her, putting her off her feed, giving her nightmares. She told Tommy because she could no longer keep it to herself; she had to confide in somebody she

123

could trust, she said, or she'd go mad. Anyway, whatever it was she'd done, hearing about it affected Tommy the same way; he couldn't keep it to himself, so he told Eddie, but got him to swear he'd keep it to himself. It was, Eddie said, bloody dynamite.'

'Dynamite,' I said, 'that could be the motive for a double murder.'

'My very thought,' Calum said.

'I like this bit about paintings. Pure speculation, but we've got nothing else. Tomorrow I'll phone Haggard, ask him if there were any pale patches on Tim's walls, nails with nothing hanging on them.'

'And continue to watch your back,' Calum said. 'Bad enough having Skaill's sniper lining you up in a 'scope's cross-hairs but, as you just pointed out, we could be completely wrong about this other, this art caper. All we know for sure is two men with muscles and no scruples have got Tim. If they've taken him for some other reason, you and Sian could be next.'

# 10

I told Sian about Calum's warning as the Land Rover rattled down from Eleanor's bungalow to our apartment on Willis's Road. She responded with a steely look that said 'bring them on'. Once we were home and I'd opened the balcony doors to let the cool, scented air banish any stuffiness, she proceeded to fortify us for any coming fray with two mugs of steaming Ovaltine.

'If they could see us now,' I said, 'they'd realize their cause is lost and move on to less formidable opponents.'

'All sensible crooks are tucked up in bed,' she said. 'You do realize it's almost three?'

'Blame Reg. It was half-two when he got back. And I didn't think much of his excuse: 'Logged on, read emails, then began checking the movement of interest rates around the world and shifting my money accordingly'.'

'What's wrong with that? Isn't that what he does?'

'Calum,' I said, 'doesn't trust him.'

I expected her to frown and tell me I was being ridiculous. As frequently happens, she surprised me.

'I've spent the better part of two days and a night in Reg's company. I suspect this image he likes to project of an ex-diplomat skilfully juggling oodles of capital while hobnobbing with internationally important personages is very carefully cooked up, possibly phoney.'

'Well, when Calum makes a judgement, even from afar, he's rarely wrong.'

'I've said I believe Reg has created an image designed to impress. That's not quite the same as not trusting him. What about you? What's your opinion?'

'The man attacked me.'

'He thought you were one of Skaill's men.'

I hesitated, then said slowly, 'Think about what happened. Reg left us, went down to his house — then shortly afterwards Ronnie Skaill came crashing in. Time passed, Skaill left, much more time passed and then Reg returned. Looking . . . ?'

'He looked shifty. As if he was hiding something.'

'And that something could have been that Skaill started from Reg's house, and ended up back there.'

'Christ, Jack, what the hell are you saying?'

'Again, I don't know. But if you're right and Reg the ex-diplomat and financial wizard is a fabrication, then what's the real story? You know the price of property on The Rock.

126

How did he manage to buy that place on Europa Road? Where does he, or did he, get his money?'

'He told you. He . . . dabbles. Moves money. Watches interest rates.'

I grinned. 'Very illuminating.' Then I sobered. 'You know I was on the phone to Calum. You didn't hear much, if anything, but I can tell a lot of what he said was speculation. OK, so now I'm speculating, and — '

I didn't get far with it.

Sian shot up from the settee, almost spilling her drink. She was looking towards the balcony. As she did so, I realized what had attracted her attention. A car was cruising up Castle Road. No wheezing taxi, this. We both listened to the throaty growl from twin exhausts. When it drew to a halt, a door must have opened on silent hinges, for all we heard was the metallic snick of an expensive lock when it was closed. Footsteps crossed the road. Sian carefully put her mug on the table and I saw her wipe her hands on her jeans. I indicated the front door. She nodded, took a deep breath and went ahead of me. She stood on the lock side of the door, the side that opened, her back to the front wall.

We waited. Footsteps again. Slapping up the stairs. Drawing closer. They stopped.

127

There was the smallest of pauses. Then a fist banged on the door.

Sian tensed, pursed her lips; nodded. I hit the handle and wrenched open the door.

'Tim,' I said, stepping back and glaring at the grinning figure standing on the welcome mat, 'if you keep startling me like that one of us is going to die, and this secret weapon I have here is why it won't be me.'

I looked at Sian. Grim-faced, she stepped away from the wall and swung to face him.

'Impressive,' Tim said. 'Forgive me if I'm old-fashioned, but when visitors arrive unexpectedly shouldn't the lady of the house dash into the kitchen and bake a cake?'

\* \* \*

'Do you mind telling me what the hell you're doing with that?'

'It's a cane.'

'Right. Stepped malacca, silver fitting over a node, ornamental silver handle wonderfully engraved. I know what it is. And I know who it belonged to.'

'Absolutely. Same feller who owned that wonderful over-and-under shotgun I haven't managed to use yet. But I *am* using Dad's cane, and bloody useful it is too.'

'Didn't do you much good when Raven

and Pagetti slipped on the brass knuckles and climbed out of their Mercedes down at the marina.'

'I didn't have it then. Or, at least, it wasn't to hand. And, as you know my friend's names, you must have been up to your usual PI tricks.'

'DI Luis Romero knows their names. They're staying at the Elliott. He's had them checked. But what I'd still like you to tell me is what you're doing with Dad's cane.'

'He's Lord Tim of somewhere very remote,' Sian said. 'A malacca cane goes with the title, it looks suitably foppish, impresses the natives.'

'Foppish my foot,' Tim said, grinning. 'I'm using it as a means of transport.'

'Really? An expensive pogo stick? Well, I suppose it's a change from a black Mercedes.' I shook my head in disbelief. 'And what the hell d'you mean calling those two your friends? Have you looked in the mirror lately?'

His bruises had yellowed. An eye that must have been closed was now looking like a half-open mussel.

'Well, actually,' he said, 'John and Pete have done me quite a bit of good.'

'If they've knocked some sense into you, I'll gladly buy them a drink.'

'And talking of drink . . . ' Tim said, hanging his tongue out as he cast a beseeching look in Sian's direction. She smiled sweetly.

'There's what's left of two mugs of Ovaltine, going cold. Will that do?'

'Well — '

'Never mind. As good old Sherlock might have put it, the curious incident of the malacca cane has put us on tenterhooks. I'll get you something to wet your whistle, and you can put us out of our misery.'

We kept our booze in the kitchen, but Sian quickly returned carrying three mugs of black coffee — much to Tim's disgust. While waiting in a slightly uneasy silence, I'd been studying his bruised and battered countenance and remembering how he'd limped badly when he crossed the threshold. As for Tim, he had that damned malacca cane between his knees and was rubbing the silver knob as if at any moment he expected a genie to burst forth in a puff of smoke.

Which, in a way, was what happened.

'So, Tim, a malacca cane as a means of transport,' I said. 'I suppose what you mean is you're using it to carry something?'

'I was going to say aren't you the clever one,' Sian said, 'but as it belonged to your dad you probably knew it was hollow.'

'I thought it was a sword stick.' I looked at Tim for enlightenment.

'At one time, yes,' he said, 'and so not really hollow except for the slit for the blade. But some clever chap modified it: removed the blade from the handle and threw it away, cleverly enlarged the interior, then fitted threads so the silver top could be screwed nice and tight. I don't know what that craftsman intended it to be used for, but . . .'

With a few quick twists he removed the beautifully engraved silver knob, placed it carefully on the chair alongside him, then upended the cane. It needed a couple of sharp taps to free what had been rolled and pushed into the hollow interior. When it did drop out it revealed itself as a tightly rolled piece of canvas that began to uncurl on the floor as we watched.

'A painting,' Sian said. 'Oil on canvas.' She leaned forward and twisted her head. 'Could be Dutch.'

'Whatever it is, whoever it's by, the speculation I told you Calum and I indulged in tells me it must be one of Ronnie Skaill's paintings,' I said.

'Christ on a donkey.' She frowned at Tim. 'Is that right?'

'Oh yes. One of Ronnie's very *expensive* paintings,' he said.

'And I don't suppose he gave it to you. You stole it from his house — and that's what your two friends pressured you into doing?'

'Well, yes and no; I mean, yes I did, and yes they did — but they didn't. Not all pressure. Actually, it's quite complicated.'

Sian gave me a knowing look. 'But you've already worked a lot of it out, haven't you, Jack? You and Calum and that telephone speculating while I snoozed.'

'Perhaps, but speculation's guesswork, isn't it? So I wonder how close I am. Tell me, Tim, taking a massive leap from sunny Gib — '

'Misty Gib, pre-dawn,' Sian said.

'OK, from misty pre-dawn here on the Med to an incident packed evening at Liverpool's Albert dock — and skipping all that nasty violence that you really must be getting quite used to — who left your apartment first? I know it was Nick Skaill and Tommy Mack who were sent to get Skaill's money or sort you out, and I know you fought like a tiger, then legged it. Does that mean you left first?'

'Absolutely. Why?'

'Calum's been talking to Tommy Mack's brother, Eddie, and some of what he told Cal will be familiar to you because you were there in the apartment with Tommy and Nick.'

'Yeah, getting beaten up.'

'But talking, first.'

'In general, yes. About this and that. Mostly trying to talk my way out of trouble. So which bit interests you?'

'According to Tommy, Nick Skaill expressed an interest in several water-colours I didn't even know you had.'

'Well, he would do, wouldn't he? His dad's got an art collection worth millions.' Tim grinned slyly as nodded at the stolen canvas. 'Less a few hundred thousand.'

'That's wildly optimistic, isn't it?'

He grin became a secretive smile, and he tapped the side of his nose with his finger.

'OK, ignoring the possible value of the stolen painting, Nick's interest in your water-colours is why I'm going to phone Mike Haggard tomorrow. I'm going to ask him if, when the police investigated the disturbance at your apartment, they noticed any bare patches on your walls.'

Tim frowned. He was leaning back. He began drumming his fingers on the side of his coffee mug. Then he nodded slowly.

'You think, when I ran for my life, Nick Skaill took my paintings?'

'I think it would be very strange if he didn't. How many were there?'

'Four. Quite small. Ten by fourteen. Inches.'

'So it would have been easy.'

Tim nodded. 'Yes, well . . . You'll have noticed before that I was evasive about whether I was pressured by John and Pete.'

'Looking at your face,' I said, 'I don't think there's much doubt.'

'They found out I've been pally with Ronnie Skaill in the past. They knew I was familiar with his villa, and I'd left some belongings there. They decided I was the man to walk in, steal a valuable work of art and walk away whistling as if I'd just delivered the milk. I refused point blank. Christ, I'm in enough trouble with Skaill. That was when they gave me the battering that put me in hospital.'

'If you were against it when they were beating you half to death, how did they manage to persuade you to leave hospital with them.'

'They told me that if I did what they wanted, stole that painting' — he nodded at the curled canvas — 'I would be able to recover my water-colours at the same time.'

'Jesus Christ, you mean you *knew* Skaill had them all along?'

'No, not until John and Pete told me. And I don't think they knew when they visited me at the marina. If they had, they would have tried persuasion then and I'd have been spared a beating.'

I looked at Sian, frowning, thinking it through.

'If they found out after that, between smacking Tim around and visiting him in hospital,' I said, 'it couldn't have been Tommy who told them.'

Tim frowned. 'Why? The information must have come from Tommy,' he said. 'Couldn't have come from Nick, it's his dad I've robbed.'

'Yes, but that was a couple of days after Tommy had been — '

'There has to be someone else here on the Rock,' Sian cut in, 'someone we don't know about. That person must have got the information about the whereabouts of your water-colours from Tommy and he kept it to himself. It only became important when you turned out to be a stubborn fool; he passed it to Raven and Pagetti when the rough stuff didn't work.'

'Well, of course, there is,' Tim said. 'I know for a fact John and Pete are working for someone, someone with brains. A Mr Big with connections, able to get rid of stolen works of art.'

'You're keeping that painting hidden for obvious reasons — it's stolen — but where are your water-colours? You must have waltzed out of Skaill's villa with them in,

135

what, a Somerfield's plastic bag?'

'Something like that.'

'So where is it now? This bag and your water-colours?'

'They've got it, John and Pete, taken it with them to the Elliott. Valuable items are best kept separate, then if someone gets caught all is not lost. The next step is bringing them together for Mr Big. That's when he gets his first sight of my paintings. He'll positively drool.'

'You hope. Are they valuable, by famous artists — or what?'

'Well, value's in the eye of the beholder, I suppose. Or in what he can afford or is willing to pay.'

'Well, go on, would I recognize the names?'

'Hang on, let me think. There's four, one each by Dürer, Demuth, LaFarge and . . . Wyatt — no, sorry, that's Wyeth.'

'I don't know much about art,' Sian said, 'but aren't they American artists?'

'Three of them. Dürer's German.'

'Where did you get them?'

Tim grinned. 'Haven't a clue.'

'Bloody hell.' I shook my head in disbelief. 'And you carried them out of Skaill's villa, walked to the waiting Mercedes.'

'They were the camouflage that hid the theft. The malacca cane was for support, I

136

was limping because of my obvious injuries. The Dutch masterpiece was hidden inside it, so if I'd been caught coming out of Skaill's villa my water-colours would have looked like the only reason I'd broken in. And those were *my* paintings, in a common old plastic bag for all to see. They'd been stolen from my Liverpool apartment. I'd traced them, recovered what was rightfully mine.'

'Luckily, you weren't caught.'

'That's right. Everything tickety-boo. Nobody in the villa but the maid, Paquita, who recognized me and invited me in. The glamorous Mrs Skaill was probably at a cocktail party.'

Sian was shaking her head. 'Tim, if the maid knew you, isn't that a dead giveaway? You arrive out of the blue, and when you leave, five works of art are missing.'

Tim looked crestfallen. 'Well, yes, but I didn't have much choice, did I? I was looking at another beating, or a slim chance of getting my paintings back and putting them to use. Anyway, I showed her the bag when I arrived, told her I was collecting my things — swimming gear, shorts, towel, sun block — and then I toddled in. When I was leaving, I waggled the bag in the air, pulled an end of the gaudy towel out to show the maid I'd got what I came for, and off I scooted.'

'And that's supposed to fool Skaill?' Sian said drily.

'Best I could do.'

'Anyway, that's for you to deal with when the time comes,' I said. 'The point is that another reason nobody was home was that Skaill was here, on the Rock. So perhaps this other person, this mysterious shadowy Mr Big in the background who sent you to Spain, knew that.'

'Could've done. Knows what he's doing, all right.'

'And so it all worked out well.' I pointed to the malacca cane, the painting on the floor. 'If all goes according to plan, you'll sell your paintings, pay Skaill with the proceeds, his thugs will be off your back and you'll own the canoe outright.'

'In a nutshell,' Tim said.

'Except for one thing.'

He grimaced at Sian. 'A right killjoy, isn't he?'

'Two things actually,' I said. 'While you've been swanning around in Spain, doing a bit of breaking and entering, a bit of theft — nothing very serious, minor offences — the Merseyside police have been busy issuing a warrant for your arrest. It may come as a surprise to you, but Tommy Mack is dead, Amanda Skaill is dead. And you, Lord Soft Lad — which is what Ronnie Skaill called you — are wanted for their murders.'

His mouth was still hanging open when the police came hammering on the door.

# 11

'Where is he?'

'Where is who?'

Romero didn't even bother answering. He simply stepped to one side and gestured to the uniformed police officers standing behind him.

I blocked their way.

'Hold on a minute, Luis. If you're looking for somebody, then tell me their name and ask me if they're here. I'll answer truthfully, if I can. If you're not going to put the question to me, then go away, get the necessary person with authority out of bed and come back with a search warrant.'

Romero dipped a hand into his jacket pocket, brought it out holding an official-looking paper. He flipped it open one-handed with a dramatic flourish, held it up for me to see.

I didn't bother looking. Instead I spread my hands and stepped back. Big and burly, the police officers brushed past Romero with deference, me as if I was an ugly piece of furniture coated in mildew. I heard their heavy shoes clumping into the living room.

'Do come in,' I said to Romero. 'We're not bothering going to bed tonight so you might as well sit down and tell me what this is all about.'

Behind me there were no sounds of struggling bodies, no crashes, thuds or curses, no clink of handcuffs. When Romero and I entered the living room, Sian was curled serenely on the settee and the policemen were nowhere to be seen.

'They're doing the bedrooms,' Sian said. 'I expect they're poking around in my frilly underwear, the dears, probably the first they've ever seen.'

'But you are an experienced private investigator like your colleague here,' Romero said, his dark eyes flashing. 'Surely if you wore underwear it would be fashioned from kevlar to deflect the bullets of our many Gibraltarian criminals?'

I noticed that 'if you wore' and was about to take umbrage but he had already turned away and was walking purposefully towards the glass doors. He stood there, touched the glass absently, gazed out across the balcony. I looked at Sian and raised my eyebrows: silent question, what happened to Tim? She frowned and shook her head. I looked for the silver-topped malacca cane. It had gone.

The two constables emerged from the

bedroom. Romero swung to face them, a trim matador pivoting on toes and heel, his short dark jacket flaring like an apology for a cape.

The taller of the constables shook his head. 'He's not here. Must have grown wings. The only way out is by flying.'

'No.' Romero swore savagely. 'I should have been more careful, left one of you outside. There is a tall palm tree that reaches the balcony. He slipped out while Scott was answering the door. Shinned down that tree and now he could be anywhere.' He flashed me a brief, poisonous look. 'Take the car, both of you,' he said. 'There's nothing more to do here, and it is much easier for me to walk home.'

He waited until they'd left the apartment and the fading sound of their car was abruptly cut off by high stone walls as they rounded the downhill bend. Then he took a deep breath, let it out explosively and thrust his hands into his pockets as if to prevent himself from lashing out.

'We tracked him back across the border,' he said. 'He was with those two men, in that Mercedes. The men in suits, with muscles and sunglasses and that stupid, stupid attitude. We didn't stop them. Those two, Raven and Pagetti, they have done nothing other than look always as if they *have* done something. There were a lot of people about. They are the kind of brainless bastards who might have objected violently if we had tried to arrest your brother.'

'And once on the Rock, where can he go.' Romero flapped his hands helplessly.

'It is that time of night when the mind is at a low ebb and even the smallest irritation can make the blood boil. But not only are you irritating me, you are being absurd; acting like a bloody fool. When I arrive, you ask me who I am looking for, yet you know damn well it is your brother. You pretend you have no idea why I want to arrest him, when I have personally spoken on the telephone to DI Mike Haggard and know exactly what you and he discussed.'

'All right,' I said, 'so I knew why you were hammering on my door with a warrant. But Tim didn't. Until ten minutes ago he didn't know those murders had been committed.'

'Nonsense. Ignoring the fact that he is the main suspect, that he was seen at the scene of the crime, that he almost certainly and very personally and brutally *committed* those murders, they have been splashed all over the newspapers and broadcast on every news bulletin.'

'He's been in Spain since this morning, you *know* that.'

'Spain has no radio blackout, and newspapers are readily available. Anyway, what was your brother doing there?'

'Good question. He was taken there by those men. I've no idea.'

'But he was here, and he said nothing, gave no explanation?'

'He wasn't here long enough to say much. I told him about the murders, that he was a suspect. Then your man hammered on the door. The timing couldn't have been worse. I'd just hit Tim with a massive shock, and the pounding on the door told him he was one short step away from a prison cell. He took fright. Must have done — and I can't say I blame him.'

In the weighty pause that followed, Sian swung elegantly off the settee.

'I'm going to slip into something comfortable,' she said. 'If we're going to play cops and robbers, I might as well be the gangster's moll. You two, sit down and stop growling at each other like a couple of bull terriers. If you're very good, I'll then make a hot drink — tea or coffee, whichever you prefer.'

'Tea will be very nice,' Romero said, and he gave her the smile he reserved for attractive women. 'I take it black, please, with no sugar.'

Slipping out of her clothes and into a flowery kaftan I recognized as one of

Eleanor's took Sian a couple of minutes, brewing tea and carrying it in on a tray a couple more; she'd filled the jug and switched on before changing. By then Luis Romero and I were sitting in two of the easy chairs, each of us lost in thoughts which I knew would run on parallel tracks but be viewed from different perspectives.

With cup and saucer on a small occasional table by his knee, and shortbread biscuits on the main coffee table so we could all reach them, it was Romero who kicked off again. He must have been sneakily reading my mind.

'The last time we spoke, at the Copacabana,' he said carefully, 'you were having reservations about a certain matter.'

I glanced at Sian. Had I told her? I couldn't remember. I knew that the reason I'd expressed doubts about testifying when I talked to Romero was because my Soldier Blue was missing. Now . . . well, I knew exactly where she was, but she certainly wasn't out of danger.

I looked at Romero, wondering how much to tell him, decided to go the whole hog.

'Since we spoke,' I said, 'I've had a special offer.'

I told him about Skaill's visit to Eleanor's bungalow, the deal he had proposed, the threats he had used to make the offer one I refused at my peril. That last bit amused Romero.

'What is he talking about?' he said. 'You are not JFK, this is not Dallas. In Gibraltar an assassin does not need a rifle, he needs a pistol which he can use at close range in an alley. This man Skaill, does he have illusions of grandeur? See himself as the godfather of an international criminal cartel? I don't know what to call this web of intrigue he is weaving, but I am quite certain it adds up to a whole lot of nonsense.'

'Rifle or pistol or a simple clonk on the head with a blunt instrument, the point is I'm a dead man if I turn him down.'

'That has always been the case. You knew that when you reported what you had seen: Nick Skaill running away from Lagoon Deep with a gun in his hand.'

'Or what, with hindsight, I perhaps mistakenly thought I had seen.'

I caught Sian's swift glance. It was the first time I'd expressed doubts in her presence, and knew she wondered what the hell I was doing back-pedalling.

I shrugged. 'I do know I then went into the club and saw a dead man.'

'Bobby Greenoak. A policeman who was under investigation for certain . . . irregularities.'

Romero let that sink in, watching me with eyebrows slightly raised as if expecting a reaction.

'Which means that . . . ?'

'It is something that perhaps makes your evidence a fraction less important.'

'I'm intrigued. How does it do that?'

'Nick Skaill probably had motive. If true, then the finger of suspicion would already have been pointing in his direction before you spoke up.'

'Well, well.'

I thought about that, and felt extraordinarily chuffed because I knew it meant Romero was still actively investigating, was not letting a conviction hang solely on what I had witnessed.

'Another thing that would help immensely,' I said, 'would be the gun. But you haven't found it?'

'It is the first thing he would have got rid of. Next, it would have been the clothes.'

'Because of . . . blood? Firearms residue?'

'Greenoak died almost instantly so there was very little blood, and Skaill would not have been close enough anyway. So, yes, residue.'

I frowned. 'I saw photographs taken soon after he was arrested. He was wearing jeans, a black T-shirt — which is what he was wearing when I saw him.'

'They are his standard leisurewear. We found several of each hanging in his wardrobe.'

'But none with firearms residue?'

'No. Perhaps he got rid of those he was wearing. And there was no residue on his skin, in his hair. But of course, we did not arrest him for two hours after the killing. By then, a hot shower . . . ' Romero spread his hands. 'Incidentally, the bullets taken from Greenoak's body indicate that the weapon used was a Walther PPK.'

I nodded. 'So what about this motive? How does it connect to Greenoak's indiscretions, off-colour deals or whatever it was he was up to?'

'It had nothing to do with his irregularities, much more I think to do with Nick Skaill's way of life. You will forgive me,' Romero said, 'if I am unable to explain further.'

I sighed. 'And now Nick's out on bail. Isn't that risky?'

'Less risky here than most other places. We're holding his passport, he's so well known in Gib there's no chance of him booking a flight anyway, and if he did somehow manage it he'd never make it to the plane.'

'Where's he staying?'

'At his father's apartment. Skaill owns a place down there on the waterfront. He has naturally made it available to his son, and

Nick has been staying there for some time. It is where we found his clothes — but not the right ones.'

'Well, I don't share your confidence. At any one time there's at least a dozen cargo vessels out there in the bay, some of them anchored off Algeciras. Money changes hands, a scruffy fishing boat casts off from Eastern Beach, Catalan Bay, an extra hand on board . . . '

'Yes, well, it was not my decision to let him out of the cell.' Romero frowned. 'But, getting back to what we were talking about, this dilemma you're facing. There was the sudden absence of your womenfolk, which was worrying but a false alarm, and that cruel method of forcing you to retract your statement is one avenue still open to Skaill. From the beginning there was the possibility of a threat to your person, which Skaill has now put into plain language, and to your face. So, with several very real threats still in place, are you any closer to a decision, to making up your mind one way or another?'

'Don't even ask,' Sian said with a withering glance in my direction. 'He knows damn well if he lets Nick Skaill get away with murder, there'll be another murder committed, much closer to home.'

Romero was watching me with amusement. 'I spoke harshly,' he said, softening, trying a different tack. 'I said that your brother had committed those murders, when even I know that a man is innocent until proved guilty. If new evidence comes to light, then, of course, it will be investigated, evaluated. But this, this Skaill business, this magical production of a killer like a rabbit out of a hat. It would instantly get your brother off the hook, but does it not appear to you to be too good to be true?'

'Actually, I believe him,' Sian said. 'But only partly. I believe he'll produce a person, but that person will have been delivered to him by . . . well, by another person. And the person delivered won't be the killer.'

Romero frowned. 'I am mystified. I cannot see — '

'Sian always talks like that,' I said, 'when she's missing her sleep — '

I broke off.

Above the clink of Sian's cup as she placed it on the saucer, the distant chirping of crickets, the muted purring of the fridge-freezer, we had all heard the thump of something hitting the front door.

Something heavy. Something soft.

And when I looked at Luis Romero and saw the light of understanding in his eyes, I knew that a night that already seemed interminable was far from over.

# 12

## Dawn

The various crime scene personnel had come and gone: the police doctor, the photographers, the men with their fingerprint kits, the SOCOs who had pottered about in their white suits and eventually, under instructions from the senior police officer, left without sealing off the landing because the sixty square feet or so of empty space where no crime had been committed had been gone over with a fine tooth comb and nothing raked up.

A young woman journalist must have been ambulance watching, usually a thankless task in Gibraltar, which was practically a crime-free zone. Tonight she'd struck lucky. Tomorrow the news of the grisly package dumped on my doorstep would be in the local newspapers and, if her star was in the ascendant, in the UK newspaper that offered her the most cash.

The body had been taken away, in a body bag. Because, of course, it had to be a body, this delivery that Skaill's men had made. If a

151

man with all his faculties had been handed over as a killer, he would have screamed his innocence even if as guilty as hell. A dead man, on the other hand, could say nothing but would nevertheless tell a story to those skilled at reading the signs.

What Skaill hadn't realized was that, by skilled personnel, signs can be interpreted in a number of ways. Or perhaps he had, and was playing some obscure double game. Who could say?

DI Luis Romero had stayed behind.

He had been interrupted with his tea unfinished. When the heavy thump on the door had startled each one of us the DI had jumped up with such single-minded purpose that he had smashed his cup, spraying the floor with tepid liquid. So with the apartment again silent he had stayed behind to apologize, to graciously accept a refill from a freshly made pot of tea — looseleaf, not bags, and with a slice of lemon — and to discuss with Sian and me the signs that had so carefully been prepared for him and his men and which he was already looking at with open scepticism.

'A point I should make about this man Skaill,' Romero said, 'is that he is acting out of character. We know he was a bad boy when younger, we suspect that there are bad boys in the UK working to his instructions and siphoning profit from illegal operations into Skaill's various bank accounts. But Skaill himself has been clean for years. Not one single black mark.'

'I said something the same to Tim about an hour before he got beaten up,' I said. 'Or, if I didn't say it, it was certainly on my mind.'

'But now he is active,' Romero said. 'Clearly, the change has come about because his son is in danger. But it is my opinion that Ronnie Skaill is out of practice, or that he is floundering because what he is encountering is outside his experience. And so what he does, what he is doing, has not fully been thought through.'

'Only a fool would say in advance that he's going to deliver a body — then do it. So he's either a fool, or very devious.'

'What he said to you was that he would deliver the killer. There was no mention of that person being dead.' Romero grimaced, shook his head. 'If that was put to him, he would deny saying *anything* to you, and he would certainly deny any knowledge of how this man arrived on your doorstep. But, that is all academic. I am quite sure that he left the Rock very soon after talking to you.'

'Mm, well, if he spoke to Nick before leaving, I know what his son would have said.

153

He'd have told him bluntly to stop messing about and get rid of that nosy PI.'

I could see, from Romero's face, that he could not understand why I had not already been coldly and clinically removed. He saw me watching him, shrugged, and gestured towards the door and the empty space that lay beyond.

'Well, Skaill has read the reports in your UK red tops,' he said. 'And for our entertainment if nothing else he has produced a likeness for us to view.'

I nodded. 'Tall man. Lean. Jeans, faded denim shirt. And the leather jacket.'

'Bloodstained,' Sian said.

I frowned, trying to jog my memory. 'I'm sure I've seen him before, you know, the dead man — but I'm damned if I can recall where or when.'

'There was no identification on the body,' Romero said. 'No wallet, no credit cards. No passport. We have no idea who he is.'

'But from my quick glance I'd say he was shot in the back of the head — right, Luis?'

Romero nodded. 'Small calibre pistol. The bullet is still in there, but without the gun . . . ' He shrugged. 'And what were you saying before we were rudely interrupted? That you believed Skaill, but that the man he was going to hand over would not be the

154

killer. So, are you still of that opinion?'

Sian pulled a face. 'Well, if it has been faked he's paid some attention to detail. I mean, that leather jacket had blood all over the front, didn't it? Which is what would happen if this man had stabbed one person while close up, then cut another person's throat.'

'And I'll bet it matches Amanda Skaill's blood group,' I said. 'And Tommy Mack's. DNA testing will prove beyond doubt that it was those two who bled copiously down the front of that leather jacket.'

'Still means nothing, does it?' Sian said.

'All it means is that the jacket could be the one worn by the man who murdered those two in the fairground,' Romero said slowly. 'What it does not prove is that the dead man inside the jacket is the killer.'

'I *know* Tim is innocent,' I said. 'I'm also convinced that Skaill, or somebody connected with Skaill, is playing a game with us. But that brings us to the obvious question. If that man in the body bag isn't the killer, and the blood samples can be matched to the victims, where the hell did Ronnie Skaill get the jacket?'

\* \* \*

155

Two hours' sleep is never enough, and breakfast saw Sian and I out on the balcony in bright early-morning sunshine, bleary-eyed, slumped in plastic chairs and munching bacon butties washed down with ice-cold orange juice. Which, as you'll know only too well if you've ever done it, leaves a coating of hard grease on the roof of the mouth. That called for hot coffee. We both held out for as long as we could, which in my case was about thirty seconds.

'That's it,' I said, as I headed for the kitchen. 'And, by the way, you're not coming with me to the Elliott.'

'I didn't know you were going to the Elliott,' Sian said when I returned with the cafetière, two mugs and a basin of sugar. 'Moving in, are you? Tired of my company? Or my cooking? Or is it my superiority? Besides, isn't that place a bit expensive for you? And anyway, where's the milk?'

'I need a name, that's why I'm going. And black coffee helps one stay awake,' I said, pouring. 'Sugar gives one energy.'

'To keep up with you,' she said, 'one needs energy like one needs a hole in the head.'

She stopped, hand to mouth.

'Have I said the wrong thing?'

'Definitely,' I said. 'As we've already seen a man who's got one, and I've been warned that I'm likely to get one, I think that's quite enough for holes in the head when it's' — I glanced at my watch — 'not yet seven-thirty on a beautiful sunny morning.'

'Change the subject then. We were both too tired to think never mind talk when we tumbled into bed at whatever hour it was, so you'd better ask me now what happened to Tim.'

'I probably know as much as you do. There was a loud banging on the door, I went to open it and, seeing his chance, Tim bolted for the balcony, vaulted the railings and slid down the convenient tree.'

'Taking with him one malacca cane.'

'And a valuable canvas. Which was last seen slowly uncurling on the floor. Where did he put that?'

'Stuffed it inside his shirt.'

'And he was nervous, and very excited. So, up for sale in the next few days will be one masterpiece, crumpled, sweat-stained and evil-smelling.'

I sipped the hot coffee, felt the grease melting, looked across flat roofs where washing hung almost motionless in the hot air to the sparkling blue water.

'He can't be on his boat. That's the first place Romero's boys would look.'

'But he knows that, and they know that he

knows that, so they won't expect him to be there and they won't bother looking.'

'So you think Tim's on the canoe?'

'I think it's quite likely.'

'OK, then when we've finished here, you can drive down and investigate.'

'I see. You mosey down to the Elliott like the man with no name, burst into a hotel suite with adrenaline pumping to tackle two dangerous men in dark suits and glasses. Meanwhile, I drive down to the marina in a battered Land Rover and wear my feet out looking for Lord Soft Lad.'

I grinned. 'Lord Soft Lad. Skaill may never gets another thing right in his life, but he hit the nail on the head there.'

# 13

The hour's time difference between Gibraltar and the UK only becomes significant when the day is young or old. Half an hour later, when I phoned Mike Haggard's office, I fully expected him to be still in bed or caught in traffic somewhere in Liverpool. He picked up on the first ring.

'Jesus,' he said feelingly, 'Ill Wind blowin' in at this time of day. What the hell is it now?'

'And a good morning to you too, Mike. How's your brother?'

'Haven't got a clue. So now you're on the line, if you see that DI Romero when you're poncin' up and down Main Street, tell him to get Harry to phone me.'

'Harry?'

'Yeah. Got a ring to it, when you reel it off: Detective Sergeant Harry Haggard. Full name Harold Hubert, but don't let on you know.'

I chuckled. 'OK, I'll pass on your message to Romero. And now you can do something for me.'

'Which is why you phoned.' I heard a theatrical sigh. 'Yeah, go on then.'

'The Amanda Skaill post-mortem. I know you'll have read the notes. Do you remember seeing anything there about a fairly recent scalp wound?'

'Why?'

'Scalp wounds bleed copiously. There was blood on Tim's leather jacket. He gave me a plausible explanation.'

'Over the phone, of course. Because, remember, you told me you hadn't seen him. Anyway, all that's out the window 'cos he was arrested last night, wasn't he?'

'Almost.'

'Jesus Christ. You mean he gave them the slip? Have I got to come over there and show them that waving flags, beating drums and blowing whistles is not the way to apprehend criminals?'

'It's Gibraltar, Mike, not Hong Kong.'

'Same difference. Where was he hiding anyway.'

'A private residence, as far as I know.'

'Yeah, yours.'

I could hear him riffling through paper as we talked. He stopped.

'It says here,' he said, 'that Amanda Skaill had sustained a small cut on the side of her head. *Anti mortem.*' He chuckled. 'Is that right? Sounds like someone from *The Addams Family*. Anyway, this wound appeared to be approximately seven days old, and had healed without stitches.'

'So Tim was telling the truth. It was an accident outside a nightclub. She fell against him and bled all over his jacket.'

'An accidental scratch on the scalp doesn't rule out him delivering the fatal thrust between the ribs a week later.'

'Ah, but recent amazing developments here on the Rock do now make that very unlikely,' I said.

'Developments? What fuckin' developments?'

'Ask Harry Hubert when he phones, he'll tell you all about it.'

Over his frantic protests, I thanked him for his help and put down the phone.

\* \* \*

The O'Callaghan Elliott Hotel sits with its back to Gunners Lane. The main entrance overlooks the tree-lined square visible from the Copacabana. At the desk I told the beautiful suntanned young receptionist that I was calling on John Raven and Peter Pagetti, and when she asked for my name I simply said Scott. She phoned through. Believing, as I'd anticipated, that I was Tim, Raven and Pagetti agreed to see me. The receptionist smiled, told me their room number, and I headed for the lifts.

What was my plan?

Ah. Well, actually I didn't have one. What is it they say? Wing it? As I was whisked smoothly and silently to the fifth floor, I knew that was the best I could do. I was also well aware that by following this course in the first place I was allowing myself to be swept off at a tangent. The two serious problems Sian and I needed to sort out were my forthcoming court appearance, and Tim's murder rap. This business of beatings and hospitals and paintings stolen from Spanish villas was an unwelcome bit of nonsense I could and should have walked away from.

I realized I was motionless, suspended in space, five floors up. I left the lift, located the room, knocked.

It was opened by a big man, an enormous man. The kind of man who creates his own eclipse. Black hair matched his shiny suit, and about him there was the stench of a thousand scruffy gymnasiums where men like him toil to sweat.

'Who the 'ell are you?'

The voice matched the physique. The door vibrated. The people in adjoining rooms probably looked up in alarm from their Sudokus. I couldn't see his eyes behind the

162

dark glasses. My twin reflections looked like two tiny ventriloquist's dummies.

'The receptionist phoned ahead,' I said, trying to keep a straight face. 'I'm Scott.'

'Nah — '

'It's the brother,' another voice yelled.

The big man's chin sagged just a little, as if anything thrown at him that wasn't a right hook was difficult to understand. Not caring to wait for words to reach brain, I winked at him and squeezed into the room.

It was the usual hotel arrangement of hall with bathroom off leading into a room with twin beds and television and not much more. Sliding glass doors were open, letting in dust from the balcony and some traffic hum.

The man who'd shouted was on one of the beds, reclining against the headboard. The bed seemed to be protesting silently, visibly wilting under his weight. Designer shades straddled his glistening bald head. His thick fingers were laced across his naked paunch. Bare feet, poking out of three-quarter cargo pants and dangling over the end of the bed even though he was half sitting up, were at least size fourteen and looked like flippers.

He was looking me up and down. For some reason I decided he was Raven, and the one who made the decisions.

'Tim couldn't come,' I said. 'I've no idea

163

where he is. He's on the run, wanted for murder.' I let that register, then said, 'He left the painting with me.'

'Thank Christ for that,' Raven said. 'So, where is it? I've got an appointment to keep with a short-tempered millionaire who's prepared to pay *mucho dinero* for that scrap of canvas.'

'*Stolen* scrap of canvas.' I nodded. 'And the millionaire will be the unknown Mr Big whose name I'd like to know. So let's do a swap. The name gets you the painting.'

The breath of serious frustration hissed through Raven's nostrils. Still sitting on the edge of the bed, he jerked his head at Pagetti.

The big man rolled his shoulders and took a step towards me. I whirled to face him. My feet were planted. He must have seen something in my eyes — it could only have been half-forgotten traces of long-buried flinty hardness from my days in the army when I'd been a young tough guy given to posturing. Or maybe he was finding it difficult to see through the sunglasses. Whatever it was, he faltered. Stopped in mid-stride, he looked uncertainly from me to Raven.

Raven was watching me intently, studying my face. He shook his head at the big man. Pagetti snorted his disgust, relaxed, flexed his hands and rocked his head on his thick neck like a boxer in the corner sucking his gum-shield.

Raven rolled off the bed, a hard man running to fat. He splashed water into a glass, knocked it back in a single draught. When he wiped his mouth with the back of his hand he was nodding thoughtfully as if he'd worked something out and was happy with it.

'I get the feeling rough stuff isn't going to work with you,' Raven said reflectively. 'Must be a family trait. We beat your brother half to death trying to force him to steal that painting from Ronnie Skaill. He was still mumbling some kind of macho refusal when he was face down on the concrete spitting blood into the sea. And the stubborn fool'd be lying in a hospital bed now if we hadn't told him about his water-colours.'

'You told him about them, told him how they were stolen, told him where they were and who had them,' I said. 'But before that somebody who'd got the word from Liverpool must have realized they were a handy lever, and told you. Who was that, your pet millionaire?'

Without hurrying, he slipped his hand under the pillow and straightened up with a small automatic in his big fist. It winked menacingly at me in the sunlight. He pointed

165

it at me, waggled it, grinned and watched me start to worry.

'The shot'll be heard,' I said. 'You'll never get out of the hotel.'

'This?' Again he waggled the dinky little gun. 'I pull the trigger this'll sound like a weak fart in a thick bottle. We'll get out all right. So will you, but much later and you'll be wheeled out by the paramedics. By then we'll be somewhere else, drinking expensive single malt while haggling over a price for those water-colours and the Dutch canvas.'

'You're already haggling and not doing too well, so I'll put it to you again: a straight swap, the millionaire's name for a stolen painting. Christ, that has to be a bargain.'

'No deal,' Raven said, and he moved in on me, close enough for me to smell last night's garlic and last week's sweat.

'Damn, I just remembered,' I said, snapping my fingers, 'Tim took that malacca cane with him and, as I've no idea where he is . . .'

Raven shook his head in dismay. 'Dear me, haven't you read your espionage stories, your spy thrillers? The rule is, never change your story. Because if you do, the interrogator is forced to work very hard with the tools at his disposal to separate truth from fiction.'

'Actually, he had the painting stuffed down

166

the front of his shirt.'

'My choice of tools is limited,' Raven said, again waggling the automatic, 'but even this little popgun will make a mess of your right kneecap.'

'If the shot is going to sound like a fart in a bottle,' I said, 'you shatter my kneecap and they'll hear my screams in Australia.'

'Not if Pete sits on your face,' he said, and with practised ease and an oily metallic click he pulled back the Beretta's blued slide.

The gun in Raven's hand had emboldened the monosyllabic Pagetti. He stepped past Raven, big hands grasping. I twisted away. He seized my shoulder. I heard the bones crackle. He held me at arm's length, then clamped his other hand on my belt and threw me on the bed. I bounced once. Then Raven sat on my feet and rammed the gun's muzzle into my right knee.

'Sit on his face,' he growled at Pagetti.

Raven had my feet clamped. I usually wedge them under a sideboard, so struggling to sit up was like morning exercises. Great fun. I'd managed to get my upper body almost vertical when Pagetti smashed his clenched fist backhand into my face. I flopped down, seeing weird lights and hearing strange noises and wondering why my nose was running.

Behind the bedlam in my head I thought I could hear a heavy pounding. Suddenly my feet were free, and Raven had gone. I rolled onto my side, blinked through my tears. Action seemed to have turned Pagetti into a fast-thinking machine. Hearing Raven talking at the door, he dragged me off the bed by my feet and let me flop face down on the floor.

'Don't say a dicky bird,' he snarled.

I was lying there, groaning and bleeding into the carpet, when Raven came back into the room. He was preceded by DI Luis Romero.

# 14

'They told me you tricked your way into the room. Something about using a false name? Then when they could not tell you where your brother was hiding you became violent.'

'Yes, I'm like that,' I said. 'I always pick on blokes twice my weight because I know they'll pull their punches. Feel sorry for me, you know? Afraid they'll kill with a single blow. That's when I blind-side them.'

'So what happened?'

'I got too excited and fell over.'

'Yes, that is what they told me.'

'Lucky you arrived when you did.'

'I prefer to call it good detective work.'

'That's pure conceit, Luis. The receptionist told you where I was, didn't she?'

'Of course. She was at school with my daughter. We chatted. I asked her if Raven and Pagetti had checked out or were still using their room. She told me they were still there, and that they had a visitor called Scott.'

I nodded, and tried to sip my coffee through mangled lips.

'They had a gun,' I said through my handkerchief. 'Raven did. He was about to

169

kneecap me. I'd led them to believe that I had, or was able to get for them if they were nice to me, a small but valuable painting my brother has stolen from Ronnie Skaill's villa.'

'Tim did that? Putting himself at risk of violent retribution from a man with whom he is already in deep schtook.' Romero appeared astonished at Tim's recklessness. 'Tell me, was this theft out of choice, or under duress?'

'One thing led to another. In the end it was one of those you scratch my back situations.'

'So what form did the scratching of your brother's back take?'

'He was able to recover something that belonged to him.'

'Ah. Of course.' Romero pursed his lips. I saw instant understanding in his eyes, and belatedly remembered that he had talked on the phone to Haggard and would know about Tim's apartment and any missing items.

'If you know what he's recovered because you knew what was stolen,' I said, 'you can probably work out what's going to happen next.'

'Let's say that what came out of your visit to friends Raven and Pagetti has solved the mystery of why they are here in Gibraltar. As to what happens next, well, what about you, Jack? Your visit to those men was for a reason. Was it productive?'

'Frustrating. Now you're making it even more so. Although Tim doesn't know it, this latest caper he's got sucked into is linked to someone in Liverpool who may know something about those fairground murders. That someone has a very rich contact here in Gibraltar. I need that name, because there's a chance that if I talk to him he may let slip more information that may eventually lead me to the real killer.'

Again, Romero was smiling. '*Someone. Something. May let slip. May eventually lead.* You have boundless enthusiasm for your brother's cause, yet these leads you are following all sound so vague, so tenuous.'

'Yes, well, Raven and Pagetti would tell me nothing, I wouldn't trade, and the situation became ugly. And now I can see by the smug look on your face that at the mere mention of works of art you've flicked through the Rolodex in your subconscious and come up with the name I need desperately. And which you are going to keep to yourself.'

'Leading to considerable frustration,' Romero said, and he grimaced to signify his regret. 'Let me simply say that we have been after this person for some time. It is possible that now, thanks to your brother, we can catch him red-handed buying works of art we know for sure have been stolen. I'm sure you will appreciate that if this name you are seeking is relevant to ongoing police investigations — '

'Yeah, yeah,' I said, grinning and ruefully accepting his refusal to divulge sensitive information to a private dick. 'But now I've told you what Raven and Pagetti wanted and what I was after, how about telling me what you were really doing in the Elliott. You've been getting more and more impatient. I can see anxiety in your eyes, the sheen of sweat on your brow, so what's going on, Luis?'

He was staring across Main Street and up Library Road. I thought he was watching the canopy of dark-green leaves over the square being ruffled gently by the warm breeze, but then I saw Raven and Pagetti walk away from the Elliott and climb into the black Mercedes.

'You realize your brother has no chance of getting away,' Romero said.

'Tim is not a cold-blooded killer — '

'Then that will be decided in court. What I am stressing to you is that there is this warrant for his arrest, and he will be apprehended. We know he is not at his mother's house, we know he is not hiding on *El Pajaro Negro*. Those places have been checked, or searched — although your mother objected strenuously, and she was backed up by Fitz-Norton who is of the opinion that he has some authority.'

172

I smiled. '*Is of the opinion*, as in opinionated?'

Romero shrugged. 'The net is tightening. Time is running out. You understand what I am saying?'

'Yes. You're doing your job. I'd expect nothing less.'

He was still watching the black Mercedes.

'They no longer interest me, Raven and Pagetti,' I said absently as, with the muted drone of a powerful engine, they drove away. 'Even if they're having one last stab at finding Tim and the painting, Sian will make damn sure they don't succeed. Just as she'll make damn sure Tim stays one step ahead of the police.'

Romero nodded to show he was listening but, like me, his mind was elsewhere.

'I was at the reception desk in the Elliott,' he said, at last answering my question, 'to find out if DS Haggard had moved into his room.'

I raised my eyebrows. 'He's staying there too? On police expenses? You amaze me.'

Romero shrugged. 'Perhaps he is paying the difference out of his own pocket. Who knows? Anyway, he has not yet arrived.'

'Maybe he's not left Manchester. D'you know what flight he's supposed to be on?'

'I know what flight he *was* on,' Romero

said, and he stared hard at me.

I frowned, wondering what he was getting at.

'Well, go on.'

'He was on your flight, Jack.'

'Really?' My mind raced, and suddenly the seriousness of what he'd said hit home. 'But if he's been here all that time . . . '

'Exactly. You got back to Gibraltar early yesterday afternoon. Naturally we allowed him time to settle in, but we would have expected a telephone call at the very least. None came, and by now . . . Well, by now he has had the rest of yesterday, all of last night and most of this morning. I anticipated seeing him first thing today. When he did not arrive at my office, I checked with the airport. We know for sure he was on that plane, he certainly came through customs — '

'Bloody hell!'

'You know something? I have jogged your memory?'

'Damn right you have. Talking about airports and planes has done it, but in one hell of an unexpected way. The dead man dumped on my welcome doormat last night, remember I told you I'd seen him somewhere before? Well, it's come back to me. He boarded the Monarch flight in Manchester, squeezed his baggage in the overhead rack

174

— and sat by me. That's right, we were elbow-to-elbow all the way. I can smell his aftershave now. I must have noticed it last night when looking at the body, they say smell is the sense most closely linked to memory.'

Romero was tight-lipped. 'So you think . . . ?'

'What, that the dead man is Harry Haggard? No, I'm not suggesting that at all. God forbid. The point I'm making is that we can now easily find out the dead man's identity. His seat number would have been on his boarding pass, I don't know if the airline keeps a record of those things — '

'I will find out.'

He was brusque, in a hurry. Coffee cups rattled on the table as he thrust his chair back and got carelessly to his feet. I pushed away my cup with the bloodstain on the rim that looked like lipstick, and was standing up a little unsteadily when I was struck by an idea.

'There is another way that might be quicker,' I called as Romero moved away and slipped into the streams of holiday-makers and tourists wending their way along the pavement into town. 'There's usually a courtesy coach waiting at the airport to take passengers to their hotels, if you can locate the driver he may have seen — '

He lifted a hand in acknowledgement, then

he was gone. I sat down heavily. My face was aching intolerably. I ordered another cup of coffee, and asked for two paracetamol. I almost scalded my mouth swallowing them, mostly because I wasn't thinking. Or, at least, not about what I was doing. In less than a week I'd gone from being the proprietor of a security firm that was ticking gently into oblivion, to a man beset by troubles coming at him from all directions. I desperately needed to sit down with somebody and talk everything through, but Sian could be, well, just about anywhere.

It all depended, of course, on whether she had found Tim at the marina. Was that likely? Would he have had the nerve, or perhaps the nous, to stay aboard the canoe, believing it to be the last place the police would look? In the end I decided that, yes, he was crazy enough to do just that, but if so then how could Romero's men have missed him when they searched the boat from stem to stern? Or had the wily DI been fishing, knowing his men had been nowhere near Tim's boat but hoping that by saying they had he'd shock me into letting something slip?

At that moment I didn't know if the plot was thickening, or becoming so thin it was slipping from my grasp. Maybe it was the bang on the nose. Is there such a thing as nose concussion? Or is harbouring such thoughts the way madness lies?

I couldn't help smiling to myself, which brought some curious looks in my direction and seemed to compound the problem. Damn it! All I knew for sure, as I once more climbed to my feet, was that the only way of finding out if Tim and Sian had been anywhere near the boat was to go down there and have a look.

I paid the bill for the drinks — Romero's included — then left the Copacabana and hurried to the nearest taxi rank.

# 15

'The police have been here.'

'And?'

'Luckily, I got here before them. I told Tim he might as well try to hide in a sardine can as on the bloody canoe. He'd made it through what was left of the night, but *mañana* is *mañana*, the police would have finished their cornflakes and it was time to move fast or be prepared to roll over and kick his legs in the air.'

'So what did you do?'

Tim, unshaven, untidy and looking tired, was grinning. 'The folk on that boat a couple of berths down the line party every night. And they've got a soft spot for me since they tripped over my bruised and bleeding body. We locked up here, left the canoe impregnable and tried to climb aboard the jet set's gin palace without rocking the boat. The doors were open. Everyone was still snoring. We sat among empty liquor bottles and ashtrays full of cigarette and cigar stubs in the panelled and carpeted salon and watched through portholes as the police clambered all over my big black bird trying to find a way in.'

'So there we were, a couple of sneaky curtain twitchers,' Sian said, 'when a big man dressed in a striped nightshirt and stinking of money came yawning in from one of the staterooms.'

'Over glasses of chilled fresh orange juice which he conjured up from what I suppose you call the galley, I told him a cock and bull story,' Tim said. 'It was along the lines of the men who'd beaten me to a pulp returning unexpectedly, we'd called the police on the mobile while fleeing, and they'd told us to stay out of the way while they dealt with the situation. His yacht, I told him, was the nearest place of refuge.'

'Lord Soft Lad,' Sian said, 'acquitted himself well.'

'Lord who?' Tim said, looking from Sian to me, uncertain whether to smile. 'Oh, and that feller on the yacht, he knows Reg.'

'Does he now? Well, nothing suspicious in that, I don't suppose. What's his name?'

'Er . . . Girard I think. Probably got Napoleon or something similarly Froggy stuck on the front of it.'

'Shouldn't that be Froggish?' Sian said.

'What it should be is politically correct,' I said, 'but never mind. The point is you've forsaken the gin palace and you're back on the canoe, Tim, but you can't possibly stay

179

here. The police probably went away to get one of those battering ram devices. They'll be back, and when they arrive you should be elsewhere.'

'I've run out of ideas.'

I looked at Sian. 'Did I ever tell you about RE Chambers?'

'Yes. You get there by following the road round Europa Point. It's a system of huge man-made caves used by the Allies during World War II, then by the Royal Engineers as workshops and storerooms when they were busy using silver bullet rock drills to turn Gibraltar into a hunk of Gorgonzola.'

'As a temporary hiding place,' I said, 'while we strive manfully, and womanfully, to clear Tim's name, I can't think of a better.'

'Forget it.' Tim shook his head. 'As far as I know there are massive metal doors with equally massive locks.'

'There's always a way in. We'll move you there later today when the coast is clear.'

'You make me sound like a big fat dirigible being manoeuvred into a hangar by tractors.'

'What you do sound like, and look like,' I said, 'is a man who is remarkably cheerful for someone facing a life sentence for murder.'

'Ah, well, that's because Lord Soft Lad doesn't describe me accurately,' he said, and he winked broadly at Sian. 'Deal with one

180

thing at a time is the way to go. Right now the priority is getting Skaill off my back. Getting the money to pay him for this sleek vessel before he removes me from the map.'

I nodded. 'But hasn't that scheme stalled? You've got the stolen masterpiece but can't go anywhere with it, and Raven and Pagetti have got your water-colours. What if they decide you're out of it for good, sell your water-colours to the unknown millionaire in lieu of the Dutch master and pocket the proceeds?'

'They wouldn't do that.'

'Bollocks. I saw them drive away from the Elliott so they've probably already done the deal.'

'Haven't you forgotten that?'

I looked where Tim was pointing. The malacca cane was propped against one of the ban-quettes.

'Damn it, no, that's what I'm saying — '

'Yes, but what I'm saying is that without it, John and Pete are stuffed. This rich collector wants *that*. He's not going to take *anything* in lieu.'

'OK. Right, so your two so-called friends must be hunting high and low for you, which is all the more reason to get you safely tucked away.'

'But in the meantime,' Sian said, 'while we wait for darkness to fall, what do we do with him?'

'Shove him in the bilges, or the engine room, or whatever's down there,' I said, grinning. 'If the police come back all they'll see is a carpet and us sitting in easy chairs.'

Tim was opening his mouth to continue protesting when my mobile rang. It was Romero. I shot a warning glance at my companions, and put a finger to my lips.

'Tell me,' Romero said, 'have you heard from your brother?'

'No, he hasn't been in touch.'

'Where are you now?'

'Enjoying a coffee in Sacarello's with Sian,' I said, and lifted crossed fingers as I rolled my eyes heavenwards.

'You have not been down to the marina, to his boat?'

'I haven't, no, but Sian was there earlier. She told me it was locked, no sign of life.'

'So my men discovered. The door, or whatever the hell you call it on a boat, locks from the outside. A padlock. They quickly realized that unless somebody had locked Tim in there, he could not be inside.'

'So they're still looking?'

'Like I have said, if he is not found in the obvious places, then he could be anywhere. What is needed now is patience, and mine is running out.'

182

For a moment there was an uncomfortable silence.

'According to the driver of the minibus at the airport,' Romero said at last, 'DS Harry Haggard was one of the people he should have been taking to the Elliott. But that did not happen. Haggard came over and spoke to him, thanked him for waiting, but said that he was travelling to the hotel in a private car.'

'Yes, and already I'm getting a nasty feeling of *déjà vu* here. Did the minibus driver see who picked him up?'

'Unfortunately no. But he was able to describe the car. It was a black Mercedes.'

'Yes, I thought it might be,' I said. 'Did he get the number?'

'Why should he? By that time he was sitting in his minibus, idly watching as he waited for traffic to move. He had no reason to note details.'

'Still, all is not lost, Luis — '

'Unfortunately, that is where you are wrong,' Romero said. 'I went first to the airline. Monarch. They were able to show me a passenger list. Your name was there, of course. The man sitting next to you — the man you recognized some hours later in less fortunate circumstances — was DS Harry Haggard.'

'Mike did say his brother, Harry, had some strange theories about those murders,' I told Sian and Tim when I'd given them the gist of the conversation with Romero.

'Any ideas?'

'On what line Harry was following? Well, if Mike calls his brother's theories weird, they must have gone against what he believes. So it's possible Harry did have a lead to another suspect.'

'Damn it,' Tim said fiercely, 'and now he's dead and we'll never know.'

'Don't be so sure. Harry might not have been working alone. Calum and Stan Jones are doing the digging in Liverpool, so I'll tell them about Harry and his mysterious theories.' I shrugged. 'Anyway, that's something else. What's absolutely certain is you can't stay here. Romero is shrewd enough to doubt my story about supping coffee in Sacarello's and he could decide to send his men for a second look. And it's too risky to move you from the marina before dark.'

'What about Napoleon?' Sian said.

'Sitting in his stateroom sipping gin and tonics sounds preferable to water and hard tack biscuits in a damp cave,' Tim said, his face brightening. 'When we were leaving he said if I needed help all I had to do was ask. I'll take my cane and toddle along and spin him another tale of woe, ask for sanctuary.'

'Go, but be very careful,' I said. 'Your name's certain to be splashed across the front page of the local and UK newspapers, and I doubt if this Girard is a fool. By now he must know you're wanted for murder, so I wonder why he isn't handing you over to the police?'

'Because he's bent,' Sian said.

'Here's another thought,' I said. 'The other night Tim and I had been on the boat for just a few minutes when that black Merc rolled up.'

'You thought then I'd been followed,' Tim said. 'What now?'

'Well, that was one idea. But I remember a grinning Napoleon inviting us on board and, as we passed, he spoke to one of the bimbos then went below. He was pulling a mobile phone out of his pocket, and knowing what happened a short while later I'll leave it to you to work out who he was about to call.'

# 16

By the time we embarked on our third gin and tonic it was sultry late afternoon. The sun was blazing through the cabin windows and bouncing off the shiny top of the central table so that both Sian and I had permanent spots before the eyes. Or was that the drink? The thought made me chuckle somewhat woozily — or was the wooziness my imagination? The chuckle became a giggle, hastily stifled.

Sian gazed across at me speculatively, waggled her full glass so that the ice tinkled and droplets sprinkled the white carpet, then used it to point in the vague direction of Napoleon's floating gin palace.

'Wonder how he's getting on.'

'Well, if I was Tim and that bronzed ancient mariner had been up close and stroking my bruises, I don't think I'd risk turning my back.'

'I'd be more worried,' Sian said, 'about all those promiscuous giggly blondes in their skimpies.'

'You would — ?'

'If I were Tim.'

'Right, glad we got that clear, because if I

didn't know you better that would have worried me. Anyway, my brother seems to be the type that appeals to half-arsed villains who make dubious incomes in sunny climes.'

'Half-arsed?'

'Big on ideas, small on achievement.'

'Is that what you call that sleek ocean-going monster?'

'D'you mean the gin palace, or Napoleon?'

'Ha. Whatever, but I wouldn't say no to his income, dubious or otherwise. Anyway, moving on, as you and I have from time to time been intimate — as in really really close, as close as any two people can get without being — '

'One?'

'Exactly, so — and I'm not blushing — you'll no doubt have noticed that I'm in a thoughtful, questioning mood, ruminating at length on the meaning of life, and so you are probably wondering what's coming next.'

'I know what's coming next. You're going to ask me what my feelings are about the move to Gibraltar. Again.'

'And?'

I hesitated, weighing the pros and cons, looking into my warmly beating heart while contemplatively drawing a line with my finger down the condensation on my glass.

'We came here partly as a favour for a

187

friend, didn't we?'

'That's right. We met Charlie Garcia in Liverpool. His brother ran a small security firm here, but wanted to retire early. Spend long sunny days on his boat in the bay, a fishing line tied to his big toe and cans of beer in a net submerged in the cool water.'

'We thought that sounded like the ideal retirement. If we took over his business, he could become the old man and the sea and we'd have fun making loads of money in the sun.'

'Except all we've done is lose money to within an inch of bankruptcy.'

'And there's very little fun to be had checking on errant husbands, missing wives, locating stolen bicycles,' I said.

Sian grimaced. 'Riveting stuff, isn't it?'

'Work for which our army background in the SIB and special forces has made us eminently suitable.'

Sian chuckled, her warm breath misting above the cold glass.

'Which probably explains cash flow which is acting like water running up hill.' She sighed. 'And so, big boy, the verdict is?'

'I miss toy soldiers,' I said at last. 'The joy of creation, the smell of white spirit and paint, the shine of red uniforms and red boxes; the sight of the special ones standing

188

in their stone niches as they guard my stairs at Bryn Aur.'

'The stairway to heaven,' Sian said softly. 'Led Zeppelin, wasn't it? And then there's the cold wind moaning high across the Glyders and ruffling swathes of purple heather; the rush of icy water under the stone bridge over Llyn Ogwen; the mournful cry of a fox . . . '

'That sounds like your kind of thing. But much further north. Up there in the desolation of Cape Wrath, teaching callow executives how to save their own lives on tough survival courses.'

'And look what it led to. Radio programmes, a media career in the making — '

'Which didn't actually take off. And wouldn't have been you, anyway, in my humble opinion. Besides, by then we were bungling amateur private investigators getting tangled up in major crime investigations, and loving every minute of it. And I know damn well we sorely miss men like Alun Morgan in Bethesda, Calum Wick, Jones the Van — Jones the *New* Van — Willie Vine and Mike Haggard . . . '

'Ah, but you can't miss Calum, because he's on his way out here.'

'He doesn't know that — not yet. I'll phone him later. I'm hoping that by now he's made some headway, and anything else that needs

189

doing can be done by Stan Jones. I have a feeling that the decisive actions needed to clear up the crimes we're looking into will be taken here — so, when you think about it, this is where everything's happening.'

'So what's that mean? That we did right by coming here?'

'I'll say a cautious no, because what's happening here now is exceptional. Gibraltar's a low crime area. We could be white-haired oldies out there with those fishing lines tied to our toes when the next murder's committed.'

'So as well as the favour, it was mainly a yearning after the other man's grass that brought us here?'

'Yes.' I shrugged. 'That was the attraction, I suppose. Always is for people who up sticks and move to distant lands. Only here, for most of the time, any grass you can see in Gib or Spain is a drab brown.'

'And a business — even if it is called Scott Laidlaw Security — that involves the boring fitting of infra-red lighting systems more than it does chasing and catching crooks has very little to do with the meaning of life — which is the philosophical musing that started this.'

'Mm. You tend to do that. You're an initiator.'

'And now?'

'We become terminators.' I flashed a grin that was alight with excitement. 'There's a lot going on. We bring everything to a satisfactory conclusion, and then we'll see.'

'Yes, and I know what that means, too, because if I'm an initiator then you're a man of impulse.' Her eyes were bright, dancing. 'Wow, d'you notice how this has sobered us up?'

'That's because we weren't drunk,' I said. 'Just bored out of our minds.'

★ ★ ★

Luis Romero came calling when the sun had sunk below the horizon and the high cloud in mostly clear skies was suffused with layers of red and pink diffused by the light mist rising from the bay. Sian was down below splashing in the shower, I was on deck wearing a lightweight gilet and leaning on the rail as I watched the lights winking on in expensive high-rise apartments.

Romero parked where he could, and walked without haste along the row of luxury yachts towards Tim's more modest vessel. Was it my imagination, or did he give Girard's gin palace a much closer scrutiny? And if he did, was it because he was impressed by glittering opulence and the heady scent of money that made its expensive neighbours smell like cheap aftershave by comparison, or because he was there in answer to another of Girard's telephone calls?

I didn't think much of the telephone idea. If Napoleon *was* involved in shady art deals, Tim — without realizing it — was useful to him, and that use didn't terminate until Skaill's painting was sold. As Tim had fled with the painting in his possession, the last thing Girard needed was Tim locked in a cell.

Barefoot, I stepped down off *El Pajaro Negro* as Romero proved the telephone idea was nonsense by walking straight past the gin palace. He approached Tim's boat with a faint smile, but a look in his dark eyes that told me I was not in his good books.

'One of my men discovered that you had been looking after this yacht while your brother was away. A caretaker has keys. Why didn't you tell me?'

'Slipped my mind. Anyway, it would have made no difference. After coffee in Sacarello's — '

'You have not been to Sacarello's. I have just left there. Nobody remembers you or Sian.'

'They probably employ part-time staff. That always leads to confusion.'

'Perhaps they do, but it really doesn't matter,' Romero said. 'I admit I am disappointed in you, and feel that I have been treated shabbily, but that is neither here nor there. Go on. You were saying, after this mythical coffee . . . ?'

'After coffee I got my keys, and we came down here and opened up. No sign of Tim.'

'And no dead body, no bloodstained knife cast aside?'

I thought he was harking back to the scene of the fairground murders, and I suppose, consciously or unconsciously, that's what he was doing. But that was not why he had come down to the marina.

'The lawyer who will be Nick Skaill's defence counsel came to see me,' he said, 'but it was Ronnie Skaill he wanted to talk about. The lawyer's name is Gomez — but, of course, you remember him; we saw him on Main Street with his slippery client. So, anyway, now he informs me that Ronnie Skaill is anxious that we should know the truth in this matter of the dead man, Detective Sergeant Harry Haggard. Ronnie says he has been duped. Taken in. Made to look a fool. Worse, he has been made to look like a criminal.'

'Goodness me,' I said, 'whatever next?'

'Yes, well, stranger things happen at sea,'

Romero said, smiling through a thin veil of cigar smoke. 'Apparently Skaill was told by somebody he trusted that the man who murdered his daughter in that Liverpool fairground had from time to time worked for him, and was either living in Gibraltar, or here on a brief visit. Skaill got this story from a person, let us call that man Mr X, and, of course, he was filled with joy at the news — these are the lawyer Gomez's words, by the way, not mine. Without asking for the killer's name, knowing that he must abide by the law — '

'Well, there's a first.'

' — Skaill told Mr X to go to Gibraltar, seize the fairground killer and hand him over to the police. At this point, however, Skaill admits he saw a way this handover could be used to his advantage. Handing over the killer, he realized, would let Tim Scott off the hook and put you forever in his debt. In a nutshell, he saw a way of saving his son.'

'Mm. Skaill sent Mr X to Gibraltar to pick up the fairground killer and hand him over to the authorities, then came to me with his offer.'

'Of course. He admits he did that, and he has no regrets. However, he swears that he was never told the fairground killer's name, and if he had known that a police officer would be murdered he would, of course — in his words — have been outraged and would have sent Mr X on his way with a flea in his ear.'

Romero had been pacing as he talked, one hand behind his back. Now he stopped, and swung to face me.

'You do realize what this means?'

'Yes, I do, and it's not pretty. There's somebody out there a lot smarter than Ronnie Skaill, and it's somebody who's got it in for him.'

'Who perhaps saw the chance of killing two birds with one stone,' Romero said.

'Harry Haggard and Ronnie Skaill. Haggard was getting close to the truth, and his was a straightforward execution. And for some reason unknown to us, Skaill was meant to take the fall for his killing.'

'It means all of those things, yes,' Romero said. 'But this complicated business also holds more important implications.'

'Oh yes. Mr X must have provided the leather jacket. But if he could so readily come up with the jacket, then he either *does* know the killer — '

'Or he *is* the fairground killer,' Romero said. 'Which leads us to another inevitable conclusion.'

'Ronnie Skaill knows Mr X. Therefore Ronnie Skaill knows the fairground killer. Without realizing it, he knows the identity of the man who murdered his daughter, and Tommy Mack.'

# 17

'Get down to the travel agent first thing,' I said, 'and book yourself a holiday in the sun.'

'Aye, and I can imagine the kind of holiday that will be. I've heard of sun and sangria, but isn't Gib the place old colonials go to knock back the gin and tonic and grumble incessantly about the damn memsahib?'

'Old colonels? Could be, but the Rock Hotel's not Raffles, and our apartment's not the Rock Hotel. Anyway, there's only the one bedroom so I've spoken to Tim and you can stay aboard the canoe — '

'Clearly I'm missing something here. The last time we spoke young Tim was being transported across Spain by a couple of thugs.'

'I'll tell you when you get here. Meanwhile, what, if anything, have you discovered?'

'Ah, well now, there's been a wee bit of progress on that scandalous behaviour that had been haunting young Amanda Skaill. I'd talked to Eddie Mack, as you know, but he was either reticent, had told me all he knew, or was scared witless. So I put on my thinking cap and decided that if Amanda had wanted to step into the confessional, she'd make sure

197

it was Eddie's wife on the other side of that fancy little screen.'

'Woman to woman,' I said. 'Always the best way.'

Sian had stopped rubbing her hair, and was watching my face.

'I spoke to Mrs Mack. She was impressed by my greying beard, probably thought I was the Archbishop of Canterbury doing his rounds. She was quite willing to talk, confidentially.'

'A confidence which you are now about to break.'

'You can't have it both ways, pal. I either talk to you, or I don't, so do you want to know or not?'

'Go on, get on with it.'

'Aye, well, maybe it's me being reticent now, because the subject that came up is one of those unmentionable taboos. At risk of offending your sensibilities, the word that was shot at me like a poison arrow from the blue was incest. As in sexual intercourse with those closely related, and young Amanda Skaill being involved in, or subjected to, by persons who remain unnamed.'

'Christ,' I said softly.

'Not only that, but young Amanda had had enough. She'd decided to open the door to the cupboard and let out all the dark secrets.'

'It was hidden,' Tim said. 'In one of those huge pots of vegetation Girard has in his stateroom. Or is it salon? And his name's Roland, by the way.'

He was holding an automatic pistol. It was still damp. Crumbs of multi-purpose compost clung to the grip.

'Christ, Tim, how the hell did you dig it out and pocket it with Girard watching? Or, more to the point, how did you know it was there?'

'Ah, well, we'd been playing backgammon. I was winning something like two hundred quid, and Roland stalked off to the head in a bit of a huff. That's — '

'Yes, yes, I know what the head is.'

'OK, and while he was gone I got up to stretch and tripped on one of those scatter rugs he's got strewn all over the place.'

'Nothing to do with the gin and tonic?'

'Absolutely not. I suppose I wasn't paying proper attention to what I was doing. Roland was going to have to cough up all that money, he'd doubled to try to retrieve the situation and I was in an unassailable winning position. So, with the mind euphoric I must have carelessly snagged a toe, and suddenly I was on my knees by a potted palm with my nose inches from all that damp soil. And right before my eyes, something was glittering. For a minute I thought I'd found the family jewels.'

'Why did you remove it?'

'Common sense. Taking one gun out of the armoury ups my chances of not getting shot.'

'Well, what you've found is something of much greater value than family jewels, or even bimbo's baubles. That's a Walther PPK you're holding, Tim.'

'I know. Funny place for Roland to hide it.'

'It wasn't Roland who put it there, it was Nick Skaill, and he was running from Lagoon Deep where he'd just shot a policeman.'

'How d'you work that out?'

'Romero told me the gun used to shoot Bobby Greenoak was a PPK. I remember that *Cloud Nine* was broken into on the same night Greenoak was murdered and, unless Girard was burying pistols in the potted palms as some sort of bizarre treasure hunt, the person who put it there has to be Nick Skaill.'

'And he took the booze to make it look like a robbery?'

'That's right. If the owner's counting up what's been taken away, nobody's going to be looking for something that's been brought in.'

'If this can be linked to Nick Skaill through fingerprints or DNA,' Sian said, 'you won't need to testify.'

'Nick will have wiped it before burying it, which ruled out prints,' I said. 'As for DNA . . . ' I waggled my hand, expressing doubt. 'Anyway, the immediate concern is to get this gleaming little weapon to Romero so the technical lads can get to work on it. I imagine they've still got the slugs taken from Greenoak's skull.'

Tim handed the Walther to me. I poked a finger gingerly through the trigger guard, although it was almost certainly a waste of time being fastidious.

'Actually, I've been thinking,' Tim said, absently wiping his hands on his chinos.

'Haven't I warned you about that?'

He grinned. 'The last place I want to hide is those dank caves.'

'If they're the last place, where's the first?'

'Here. On the canoe.'

I looked at Sian. 'Has he got a point?'

'Well, Romero can't keep coming back here. And if Tim stays as quiet as a mouse, reads by the light of a guttering candle — '

'Sleeps the sleep of the dead, more like it,' Tim said, 'because I can't remember when I last got the old head down.'

'I think it's a big mistake.'

Tim stared at me. 'Why?'

'To be on the safe side, we're assuming Girard is linked to Skaill, or Raven and Pagetti — '

'Or Reg,' Sian said.

Tim frowned. 'Why Reg?'

'Never mind — '

'No, hang on, dicey diplomats are two a penny, but this one's a bloke who's close to Eleanor.'

'It's not what we know, it's what we suspect.'

'We? That means you and Sian?'

'And Calum. He was the first to raise doubts, asked me could Reg be trusted. Sian spent some time with Reg, and is inclined to agree with Calum: she doesn't believe Eleanor's golden boy was a diplomat, thinks he's a phoney and on the financial fiddle.'

'But there's no evidence?'

'Well, no. But his actions are suspicious. I arrived unexpectedly at Eleanor's house, and Reg leaped on me, said he thought I was one of Skaill's men. Later he said he was going to his house to read emails, but didn't return until the early hours of the morning.'

Tim was looking thoughtful.

'When was this?'

I looked enquiringly at Sian. 'That was the night I got back from the UK, wasn't it?'

'*Last* night.'

'Really? I'm truly amazed how time flies.'

'He was here last night,' Tim said. 'Reg. At the marina. On *Cloud Nine* with Girard. He might have gone to his house first, but he was certainly here and they were discussing something hush hush. I asked, and Girard grinned and tapped the side of his nose.'

'Well, well,' I said. 'I mean, it's still nothing even approaching conclusive because all we've got against either of them are vague suspicions. But I'm more and more certain it was Roland Girard on the phone to Raven and his dense pal.'

'So what are you going to do?'

'Nothing. What I'm worried about is what you're going to do.'

'I'm staying here.'

I stared at my brother. His mouth was set in a stubborn line, his eyes defensive but determined.

I sighed.

'Right,' I said, 'so you do that. Sian and I will head into town and hand the PPK to Romero.'

'We could always lock him in,' Sian said. 'What was it Romero said, if the padlock's in place Tim's unlikely to be inside?'

Tim was frowning and shaking his head, and I nodded agreement.

'Too risky. If I'm right about Girard then he's likely to phone Raven and Pagetti, and the last thing Tim wants is to be trapped.'

'Absolutely,' Tim said, his smile serene, 'and actually I'm tired of hiding, tired of running. So, if the bully boys are going to come, let them. Last refuge, and all that rot — and as a last resort I've got Dad's over and under Verney-Carron shotgun which will make anyone's eyes water.'

# 18

In an atmosphere redolent of cigar smoke and beeswax furniture polish I gazed at Romero's antique mahogany desk in his Irish Town office, the heavy brass inkwells with their nibbed pens, the bamboo blinds looking comfortably tatty on the windows and the obligatory ceiling fan whirling lazily overhead.

In the light from a green banker's lamp, Romero was using a gold pen to scribble on a flimsy yellow pad. He didn't look up, but lifted a hand in acknowledgment and continued writing. Without saying anything I placed the blue-black Walther PPK on the desk in front of him, in line with the top edge of his desk blotter. It made a hard, edgy sound. I saw his eyelids flick up and down.

He put the pen down carefully, lifted his head and sat back.

'Where did you get that?'

'Tim found it on board *Cloud Nine*. That's the big luxury — '

'Yes. I know *Cloud Nine*, we know Roland Girard. If you must know, it is the name you were looking for, the man we know buys works of art, the man we are now hoping to catch red-handed buying your brother's paintings.' There was a cynical twist to Romero's lips. 'Tim found this Walther PPK, and handed it to you. What about Girard? What did he have to say by way of explanation?'

'He doesn't know it's been taken, and I'm pretty sure he didn't know the gun was where Tim quite literally stumbled across it. The picture I have is of a killer running from a nightclub, and an opportune night-time break-in done for reasons other than theft. Nick Skaill. And he's been unlucky. On that boat, with those people, the gun could have remained hidden for years; might even have gone down at sea with all hands.'

Romero must have pressed a hidden bell push. A detective in shirt sleeves came soundlessly into the room. Romero pushed the PPK towards him with the cap of his gold pen. The man nodded, picked it up with a handkerchief and went out with as much disturbance as a warm draught.

No words were spoken. Romero shrugged when he saw the question in my eyes.

'He knows what to do. No prints will be found anyway, and tests for DNA take longer than most people realize. But there are also ballistic tests, and in the meantime, of course, Girard will be questioned.

'With the discovery of the weapon the Nick Skaill case has moved on,' I said, 'and now I'd like to talk about another.'

'Steady The Buffs,' Sian said softly, knowing at once where I was going.

'I'm trying to come up with somewhere safer than where he is now,' I said with a glance in her direction. 'This is the best I can do.'

'Promising,' Romero said, who was also no slouch at catching the drift. 'But, do go on, the floor is yours.'

'You've been trying to arrest Tim, on instructions from the Merseyside Police who have been prompted to act by what is mostly circumstantial evidence.'

'What about the knife?'

'Too obvious, too easily planted. My colleague in Liverpool has dug up something much stronger. There is a rumour — '

'Which is useless as evidence — '

' — mentioned in a talk with a reliable female witness who has no reason to lie. If true, the rumour provides a strong motive for a member of the Skaill family to . . . eliminate Amanda.'

'Which member?'

'We don't know. But similar cases frequently lead to the head of the family.'

'Then the crime alluded to is obvious, you have no need to spell it out in sordid detail,'

Romero said. 'However, you mentioned a colleague.'

'Calum Wick. He'll be arriving in Gibraltar tomorrow.'

'Even so, from an unnamed female witness Mr Wick merely got an unsubstantiated story, an intriguing rumour. I am getting stories from all sides. What are you leading up to?'

'On the telephone, Calum was cagey. I think he'll tell a better story when he gets here, one with more substance, one that will lead to the man who will be convicted of the crime for which Tim now stands accused.'

'Suspected. He will be accused when he is arrested,' Romero said softly, 'if the evidence is strong enough for us to make a case. But, in the meantime, what is it you want me to do?'

He knew, of course. He just wanted me to come right out with it.

'With this murder rap looking ever more flimsy,' I said bleakly, 'but with men with evil intentions closing in on him from all directions, for his own safety I want you to arrest my brother.'

★　★　★

'We told him to stay in the dark,' I said, 'and read by candlelight. He's probably tucked up in bed cuddling Dad's antique double-barrelled shotgun. He'll be sensitive to the boat's every movement, and it's bound to rock when we step aboard. I think we should make some noise.'

'Tambourines would do nicely,' Sian said in a voice that wasn't steady. 'A couple of kettle drums and a fife or two. I remember when I was a kid in pigtails, bands like that used to march down the street on hazy Sunday mornings . . . '

She didn't finish. She was only talking at all because she was nervous. Since we parked close to Bianca's I'd been scared rigid by what I was about to do. *Cloud Nine* was in darkness. We passed the silent gin palace like lascars returning in a line to our rusty South-seas freighter, and walked on towards Tim's canoe with moonlight dripping cold and eerie on the concrete strip. Somewhere a chain clinked. From the moored yachts with chrome trim glittering like a thousand gun barrels, misted portholes watched us with the malevolent eyes of the undead.

Romero was leading the way. It was to him I had voiced my words of caution. He was armed, but not noticeably, and when we reached *El Pajaro Negro* and came together in a nervous bunch he lightly touched my arm.

209

'If it's your voice he hears it will cause him less alarm.'

I nodded, and took a step towards the boat.

'Tim,' I called, 'I'm coming aboard, so finger off the triggers and hold your fire.'

'Jesus Christ,' Romero said softly.

The marina's silence was like a heavy cloak outside which the faint sounds of Gibraltar town's night-life were ghostly whisperings.

I stepped on board the canoe. The deck dipped just a little. I heard the tiniest of ripples softly lap the quay. Moonlight cast shadows across the door. We'd left it unlocked. The hairs on my neck prickled when I saw the brass padlock hanging in the hasps. It was closed. I reached forward and grasped it, then closed my eyes as my heart lurched with relief. But the relief was short lived. The lock was merely hanging there, open — but I knew we hadn't put it there.

'Someone's been here,' Sian said, appalled.

She was right behind me, holding my arm tightly. Romero was with her, but had stepped to one side as she spoke. I knew he had heard her and was giving himself room to draw a weapon.

I looked at him and shook my head.

'We've been through this already. The lock's hanging in the hasp. That can't be done

210

from inside. Whoever was in there must have left.'

'So they've taken Tim with them again,' Sian said. 'Or . . . '

I took hold of the padlock, angrily threw it overboard. It splashed into the sea as I pulled open the door and ducked inside, into the warm, stuffy cabin that felt . . . wrong.

'Tim?'

Romero said, 'I can smell — '

'Cordite. Yes.'

I clicked on the light.

'Oh, God.'

Sian's voice was brittle, like ice. I stood frozen. She made as if to push past me, sensed my horror and paused to look at my face and brush my hand with her cold fingers —

'No,' Romero snapped. 'Leave everything, do not touch.'

He had stepped forward quickly and his arm was in front of us, barring the way. I rocked back, suddenly unsteady. Sian's breath was catching in her throat.

Tim was lying on his back on one of the cushioned banquettes. One arm dangled over the edge. The tips of his fingers were touching the carpet. A bottle of Jameson's stood on the central table. Alongside it, the glass from which Tim must have been drinking when he was disturbed lay on its side in a rich amber pool.

There was no sign of the shotgun. I wondered if he'd kept it close — down the back of a cushion, perhaps — but been caught cold with no chance of reaching it. And even as my gaze was drawn back again and again to my brother's body, to the horrible wound in his forehead, another part of my mind was telling me to keep looking for that elegant, gentleman's weapon that had been as much use to Tim as the malacca cane.

That, too, seemed to be missing. The cane. It had been propped against the banquette. Now it was nowhere to be seen.

Romero had moved forward, carefully, his eyes darting everywhere. But now he stopped. He went down on one knee, reached out to touch something, a wisp; let his eyes lift and follow a trail that led directly to Tim.

'Straw, put down deliberately,' Sian said. 'So this has to be Skaill's doing, doesn't it? He's the one Tim must have driven wild with money owed and paintings stolen, he's the only one who would leave this kind of message.'

She was almost certainly right, but whoever it was had come prepared. Wisps and stems of dirty straw lay across the shiny boards, across

212

the carpet, along Tim's sprawled legs and the broad chest that was forever still. The final wisp — the last straw — had been stuck in the corner of his mouth so that as he lay there he might for all the world have been a farmer's boy dozing in the sun.

But this was night, on the Mediterranean coast, there was the stink of gunpowder in the air and Tim was not sleeping. In the centre of his forehead there was a small hole surrounded by black powder burns. My brother's eyes were open, and staring, but there was no doubt at all in my mind that he had been shot dead very soon after we left him on his own.

# 19

Her tears were warm, pooling in the hollow of my throat, her hands gripping the sides of my shirt so that her knuckles dug painfully into my ribs as she shook me gently and rocked her head from side to side. When, after a few brief moments, she looked up at me, her eyes were misted, her cheeks wet, but as always with Eleanor it was not weakness that shone through, but strength.

She stepped back with a deep, shaky sigh, but still kept tight hold of me.

'It's over, isn't it?'

'Yes,' I said, 'Lord Soft Lad's gone for good.'

'Sounds complimentary, now, doesn'it? A term of affection, comin' too late. Or is that me bein' corny and sentimental?'

Her Liverpool accent and dropped consonants always became more noticeable at times of stress, and I realized now that she'd been talking that way for the past few days. She'd been worrying about Tim for most of that time, but was there something else, trouble with Reg . . . ?

'If it's any consolation,' I said, 'there's no

more wondering what he'll be up to next, when he'll turn up, what shape he'll be in, no more sticking plaster required, no salve for wounds, no rescue missions to far off places.'

'But that was in your imagination anyway, wasn'it?' she said, tenderly touching my cheek. 'Couldn't have been rescue missions, could there, because nobody ever knew where he was?'

'In my imagination, or to my eternal regret?' I said. 'I know it's what I'd like to have done. It's what I'd like to do now, but from this, this final mess, there is no rescue, no . . . ' I spread my hands helplessly, and looked over at Sian.

'So find the fairground killer,' she said bluntly. 'We know it wasn't Tim, never was, never could have been because to take a human life just wasn't in him — and even I could see that, though I met him such a short while ago. The sad thing is, Tim won't have the satisfaction of knowing he's beaten the rap.'

Busy at the drinks cabinet, Reg glanced over his shoulder and chanced a restrained smile.

'Beginning to sound like a gangster movie,' he said.

''*Made it, Ma, top of the world*',' Eleanor said softly. 'He was always reachin' for the

215

stars, Reg, but his arms were never long enough.'

'So now we take over,' Reg went on, smiling fondly at her. 'And, although this may be the wrong time to bring it up, I'm pretty sure something suspicious I saw the other night — last night, I suppose it was, or the early hours of this morning — has some kind of connection to this whole series of incidents.'

'As they say in Mesopotamia,' Eleanor said, '*au contraire*. This, Reg, is absolutely the rightest of times to start talkin' if you've tripped over a clue.'

'Perhaps you'd better tell us what you saw last night,' I said, 'when, according to your story, you were either here with Eleanor, or down at your house reading emails.'

'Wasn't exactly a story, old chap.'

'Then what was it, exactly?'

Eleanor had hold of his hand. Her eyes were moist and she was clutching a damp tissue but she was in tight control of her emotions and she didn't like my tone.

'What's goin' on, Jack?'

'When we're in PI mode,' Sian said, springing to my rescue, 'we look at a case from every angle and do a lot of lateral thinking. Seemingly irrelevant incidents often lead to a breakthrough, and we just weren't, well — '

'When Reg left here last night,' I said, as she floundered, 'we both thought he was away for rather a long time.'

'Meanin' what, precisely? Isn't that like discussin' the length of a piece of string?'

Eleanor's voice dripped ice. Reg looked mildly amused.

'And a waste of time, yes, but when talking to Tim this afternoon we found out why Reg took so long. Moored close to Tim's boat, there's a gin palace called *Cloud Nine*. The owner, Roland Girard, may have had something to do with Tim getting beaten up and stealing Ronnie Skaill's painting. Now, diplomatically' — I dipped my head to him — 'I'm going to let Reg take it from here.'

'Won't get you very far in that direction,' he said. 'Roland's a playboy dipsomaniac with inherited wealth who surrounds himself with page three girls and dabbles in art. When he was there on the boat he watched somewhat bleary-eyed through a rarely full glass as Tim staggered from one crisis to another.'

'What d'you mean when he was there? I thought he lived on board.'

'Good Lord, no. *Cloud Nine* is his playground. He lives in a luxury apartment a short way from the marina.

'He spends a hell of a lot of time on that boat. Raven and Pagetti must have been

217

summoned by phone calls from an observer who saw Tim arrive with me, and I don't like coincidence.'

'Put up with it, old chap, because it happens.'

'You mean it wasn't Girard? He didn't call the muscle, arrange the beating?'

'I've no idea.'

'What were you doing on that boat, *Cloud Nine*?'

'Minding my business, which is what I advise you to do.'

'Or?'

Reg waved dismissively with his glass. 'Nobody's going to bump you off. I supplement my civil service pension in various ways, and the details have nothing to do with you. Anyway, you're an investigator and I've already given you a clue.'

'The drunk who dabbles in art?'

Reg shrugged. 'A lucrative game, if you know what you're doing. And carefully check provenance.'

'But what if the artwork he's dabbling in now was stolen from Ronnie Skaill?'

'Then go and talk to Girard, find out what he knows. Take Romero.'

I sighed. Sian rolled her eyes. Reg, clearly, was not going to be drawn, and I was beginning to believe that the suspicions voiced by Calum would lead to little more than white-collar wheeler-dealing and a lot of creative accounting. There was nothing there to harm Eleanor, and that was my only concern.

'I think I owe you an apology, Reg,' I said, 'though you won't have a clue why. But, moving on, what was this suspicious incident you witnessed?'

'Well, you mentioned coincidence, so how about this one? It saw me driving down Trafalgar Road at the precise moment when Nick Skaill was helping to lift something bulky, floppy and very heavy over the wall out of the Cemetery onto Prince Edward's Road. They were having a hard time. You know what Trafalgar Cemetery's like, in a wooded hollow between two roads. The back of it's quite steep, and that's where Prince Edward's Road lies.'

'And this . . . thing . . . was floppy like . . . ?'

'Bluntly, like something very dead that was later dumped on your doorstep.'

I frowned. 'You sure it was Skaill? He's out on conditional bail, living in Ronnie's apartment. If he was at Trafalgar Cemetery at that time, he must have broken curfew.'

'It was Nick. I'm as sure of that as you were when you saw him running from Lagoon Deep.'

'Gives a whole new meaning to the term graveyard shift,' Sian said.

Eleanor pulled a face. 'Yes, and my Reg is an observant little sod, but it doesn't help with clearin' Tim's name.'

'No need to take my word for it,' Reg said. 'Just use what I've given you and see where it leads.'

I was on my feet as he finished speaking. Eleanor's phone was a discreet little handset by the red-shaded table lamp. It was answered almost before it had time to ring.

'Romero.'

'I have learned,' I said, 'that on the night of Harry Haggard's death, Nick Skaill broke his curfew. He was seen — '

'Nick Skaill,' Romero said, 'has disappeared. He is on the loose, roaming free, somewhere in the maze formed by the narrow back streets of Gibraltar. He has gone for a reason, wouldn't you say? I suggest you take very great care.'

# 20

## Friday

By ten o'clock the next morning I had been down to the police station in Irish Town with Reg, and he had told DI Romero the story of his night-time drive down Trafalgar Road. He was questioned in detail, but could come up with little more than he had told me: poor lighting from the main roads, definitely Nick Skaill, another man he didn't recognize, a heavy, awkward object being lifted over the wall.

Detectives had rushed to the southern end of Main Street and searched Trafalgar Cemetery. There were footprints everywhere in the soft earth, and bloodstains were found on gravestones near the wall bordering Prince Edward's Road. The samples had been scraped into evidence bags, and were being analysed. From their reading of the scene, detectives believed that the dead person who had been moved — surely Harry Haggard — had been killed elsewhere but kept hidden among the gravestones until ready to be moved.

In my opinion — and Romero agreed with me — the signal to move the body had come by mobile phone from Ronnie Skaill as he sat in his Mercedes after leaving Eleanor's bungalow. What Reg had seen was Nick Skaill humping Harry Haggard's body out of the graveyard and into the boot of his car before driving up to our apartment in Castle Road.

Which, Romero pointed out, didn't mean that Ronnie knew what was going on, or that Nick was the mysterious Mr X.

He then told me that Tim's body had been taken from the boat to the mortuary. The post-mortem would take place that day, though it was a formality because the cause of death was obvious. The body, he said with deep regret, would not be released for several days.

Nick Skaill was still missing.

We left him, cheerful, outwardly making light of the problem but facing his day with grim determination. Reg set off up the Rock to Eleanor's (his Mercedes was white, of course), assuring me that if any of the Skaills hove into view he would protect her with his skinny life. I drove my battered Land Rover up Castle Road, and by mid-afternoon it was like old home time on the ranch: Calum Wick arrived by taxi from the airport, and not caring too much for where the sun was in relation to the yard arm we settled on the balcony — in the shade of the parasol with big pink polka-dots — with ice-cold gin-and-tonic and wooden dishes of assorted spicy nibbles.

'So what's all this about Tim?' Calum said. 'Are you saying he made it back from Spain?'

'Oh, he got back OK. And we were right, he did go to Marbella to steal from Ronnie Skaill. But the Gib police tracked him when he came back across the border, and moved fast to arrest him for the fairground murders.' I shook my head. 'Tim got away, and after that, it all went pear-shaped.'

As the sun beat down on the balcony, insects hummed lazily, the spicy nibbles leaked grease in the heat and ice tinkled in frequently-raised misted glasses, I brought Calum up to date with pretty well everything that had happened since Tim walked into the apartment wearing his bloodstained leather jacket. When I awkwardly described the discovery of Tim's body on board *El Pajaro Negro*, he was lighting one of his thin Schimmelpenninck cigars, and the sheer heady familiarity of that rich aroma almost brought me to floods of tears. As he looked at my brimming eyes his grin was lopsided and understanding. He reached across the table, we clinked glasses, and in that one impulsive

223

gesture we were not mourning Tim but celebrating what he had been. A great weight lifted from my heart.

'That Frog chappie is the buyer,' Calum said emphatically when I'd finished my tale and we'd sat for a while in contemplative silence. 'That's just my humble opinion, but you can count on it. And you got it right when you spotted him sneaking below decks with the mobile phone that first night. He was dropping Tim in it.'

'Reg knows him, and is . . . non-committal.'

'Aye, well, I don't know Reg, but if he's like the civil servants I *do* know he'll be living in his own cocooned little world that bears no relation to reality.'

'Girard fits, anyway: Tim said at the start that the buyer lives in a waterfront penthouse. And as Reg deals with Girard, he'll have his address. Romero will, too; he told me they've had their eye on Girard.'

'So those two heavies . . . ?'

'Raven and Pagetti.'

'They'll be selling their wares to this Napoleon?'

'Or trying to. If I'm right and the Skaills murdered Tim, then Ronnie's recovered his Dutch masterpiece. It was in Tim's malacca cane. The heavies will be left with the water-colours, and Tim reckoned that with-out the stolen painting, Girard won't be interested.'

'Which means, unless we're desperate to recover those, we haven't really got any reason for going after Raven and Pagetti,' Sian said. 'They used Tim, but there's nothing we can do about that now.'

I looked into my drink, pensively moved the lime slice around the rim of the glass with my finger.

'What about Tim and the fairground murders?'

'I'll tell you what about that,' Sian said. 'We don't let the police take the easy way out. The way they'll see it, Tim was the killer, Tim's dead, case closed. That's an easy option, but it's not going to happen.'

'So if we let the art caper slide,' I said, 'we're left with the hunt for the fairground killer, and keeping me alive until Nick Skaill's trial — '

I broke off as there was a discreet tapping on the glass doors and Luis Romero walked out into the bright sunshine.

* * *

'I am not quite sure of the situation regarding ownership of your brother's boat,' he said.

'Can you enlighten me?'

'I haven't given it any thought. I don't know how much Tim had paid off the asking price, but at a guess I'd say it still belongs to Ronnie Skaill. Why d'you ask?'

'*El Pajaro Negro* set sail from Marina Bay an hour ago. Two of Ronnie Skaill's men were on board.'

'Did you send a police launch after it?'

'It was too late. Besides, I wanted to check with you first. If ownership has reverted to Skaill, we have no authority nor even any reason to stop it.'

'How'd you know Skaill's men were on board?'

'It was seen leaving, motoring out into the bay. The two men are known locally.'

'What about Nick? Didn't it even occur to you that he could be on board, heading for Christ knows where, never to return?'

'I told you, it was too late to do anything. Once that boat was out of the bay and in international waters, we had no jurisdiction.' He paused. 'Also, we are no longer looking for Nick Skaill.'

You could have cut the silence with a knife. Romero was standing placidly, arms folded, the circus lion tamer who's just ripped open the cage door and set the pride loose amongst the crowd. Sian lifted her glass to him,

226

waggled it in invitation. He declined with a smile and a polite shake of his head.

'He's in custody,' I said. 'Nick Skaill. Please, do not tell me he's out on bail after what Reg witnessed.'

'Fitz-Norton was wrong,' Romero said flatly. 'Mistaken, perhaps mischievous, I don't know. But Nick Skaill has an alibi for the time when he was supposedly in Trafalgar Cemetery.'

'Who gave him the alibi?'

'Roland Girard.'

'You're joking!'

'And others. The apartment Nick Skaill is using is in the same block as Girard's. There was a party of sorts. Nick Skaill was seen by, oh, half-a-dozen people at the very least.'

'Reputable?'

Romero shrugged. Straight-faced, he said, 'They are citizens who at present are not guilty of or being investigated for any offence.'

Sian was watching me, one cynical eyebrow raised.

'Nick's pals,' I said, nodding. 'End of alibi, but nothing anybody can do.'

Then my phone rang. I apologized, left them to their frustration and walked to the end balcony by the tall palm tree. I could see scrapes and gouges in the smooth bark, a broken palm frond where Tim must have hung on, and I closed my eyes and took the call with a lump in my throat.

'Yes?' I said huskily.

And I listened, stunned, as Reg Fitz-Norton topped even Luis Romero in his ability to ruin a glorious afternoon.

'OK, Reg, pour yourself a stiff brandy, then sit down,' I said. 'Have one ready for me, too; I'll be with you before you've twirled the glass and inhaled the fumes.'

I snapped the phone shut, and stood for a moment, staring into the hot, shimmering distance.

'Jack?' Sian called from the table. 'What's going on?'

I took a deep breath, and turned to face them.

'That was Reg,' I said.

'God, not Eleanor?' Sian said, and she was already scraping back her chair, her blue eyes wide.

'Reg hasn't seen her since she popped out to do some pruning in the garden. She's missing. And, after what Luis has told us, I'm pretty sure we all know where she is.'

# 21

The sun was low enough over the hills behind Algeciras to cast long raking shadows as I took the battered Land Rover across the border, rattled through La Linea de la Concepción and picked up the A7. It was one of those routes on which a confliction of bewildering number changes would see us following the A-383, the E-15 and possibly the AP-7 — though I wasn't too sure about that one. Not that it mattered. What I did know was that the A7 would eventually dip to follow the Mediterranean coast and take us all the way to Marbella.

'If you think about it,' Calum said, 'this is a race that's difficult to call.'

He was sitting in thc back seat. Sian was alongside me, half turned with her elbow on the squab so she could see both of us.

'Yes, it's sleek seagoing motor cruiser against clapped-out Land Rover,' she said. 'The motor cruiser cuts merrily through the waves at a top speed of over forty knots, whereas the Land Rover blows smoke and starts shaking itself to pieces at anything over sixty.'

'But this clapped-out Land Rover's got the benefit of fast motorways and an experienced driver,' I said with a grim smile, 'whereas Tim's boat's got a couple of thugs at the helm, and they're facing unpredictable winds and seas that'll feel like uneven concrete if they go flat out.'

'As far as mileage goes, there's not much in it,' Calum said.

'No, but against that they already had an hour's start before we left the apartment. OK, so they had to head south first and swing round Europa Point before they could point the bows to the north-east, but still . . .'

'Be interesting to get Romero's reports on progress.'

'How's he going to monitor progress?' Sian said. 'You spoke to him again before we left, Jack. What's he got organized?'

'A helicopter,' I said. 'I don't know if it's Spanish military, or one of those gaudy civilian jobs that take holidaymakers on half-hour spins — I don't know and don't care, but it will certainly be in the air by now.'

Romero, restricted by regulations, had reiterated that he could not have *El Pajaro Negro* pursued, and could not send the Gibraltar police through Spain by road. He had phoned his opposite number in Spain to report what we suspected: that a British

230

woman had been kidnapped and was being taken by sea, possibly to Marbella, possibly to a villa owned by a UK ex-pat crook named Ronnie Skaill. Then he had used some influence, called in a favour, and it was the Spanish police who had come up with the helicopter.

'Skaill's villa's in the hills,' I said, thinking ahead. 'According to Romero it lies off the A355 near a small town called Ojén.'

'Hasn't he got an address?'

'He didn't have it with him. He'll phone it through when we get close.'

'And when we do get close,' Sian said, 'when we actually get there and drive into the hills and onto this undoubtedly white villa's landscaped grounds with swimming pool set against a backdrop of palms and bougainvillea — what then?'

'Depends. The boat's got to sail into the marina at Marbella, tie up, then they have to transfer Eleanor from the boat to a car. And I know how tough my mother can be. Unless she's sedated, she's going to be one hell of a handful.'

'That's if they've got her,' Calum said. 'What if she'd needed something on the spur of the moment, and headed down to the shops? She was gardening. Maybe she needed fertilizer, a wee pair of secateurs. What if Reg

231

panicked and grabbed the phone, and is even now tearing strips off her for scaring him half to death as well as making him look a fool?'

'Oh, they've got her,' I said. 'And they're taking her to Skaill's villa because they know that here, in Spain, they're between two camps and practically beyond the law. The next step after that is to communicate with me. The business with Haggard's body was a fiasco. Skaill's now going to tell me that if I go to court to testify against Nick, Eleanor dies.'

'It's got to be a bluff,' Sian said.

'Why? And can we afford to take that risk? Anyway, the point I was about to make was that we *are* faster than the boat, they *may* have trouble dealing with a feisty pensioner, so we *could* reach the villa before them.'

'Aye, and that would make for an interesting situation,' Calum said. 'You think he'll have left the place empty?'

'Someone's got to go down to the marina to meet the boat. I think that will be Skaill.'

'Tim mentioned something about a maid,' Sian said, 'but I don't think she'll live in. If the house is empty, Calum's impressive housebreaking skills will get us inside. Once in, we'll have the advantage.'

The setting sun was at our backs. Ahead, the land was undulating and dun-coloured, with white houses and patches of bright green and always to our right the blue Mediterranean. Traffic was moderate, but fast in both directions on what I think was called the Autovía del Mediterráneo. It was a dual carriageway with two lanes either side of the central reservation, and hard shoulders good enough to look like part of the road. I'd been keeping my eye on a juggernaut that had been closing up behind us. As I flicked my eye to the mirror it roared by, buffeting the Land Rover so that I had to tighten my grip on the wheel, then almost sucking us the other way into the vacuum it was dragging in its wake.

'If we *are* ahead of them when we reach Marbella,' I said at last, as the obvious dawned on me, 'we can forget about the villa and head straight for the marina.'

'We won't know,' Sian said.

'Yes, we will, because Romero will keep us up to date. And if we get to the marina before they leave, there'll be people there, relaxing on the boats or enjoying an evening walk by the sea. With witnesses, there's no way they'll be able to get Eleanor — '

My mobile phone rang. I took it out of my pocket, handed it to Sian. She pressed the button, listened, nodded to me.

'Yes, Luis?'

Then she looked at me again, but this time

she screwed up her face in a grimace of disappointment. When, after a few seconds' conversation she thanked him and bade him farewell, she was shaking her head.

'We just lost the race, because they cheated. The boat pulled into Sotogrande harbour.'

'Damn. I know it. Or of it. It's about a third of the way between Gib and Marbella.'

'And we're almost there,' Calum said. 'Just passed Pueblo Nuevo something or other. That's coming up to Sotogrande, and close to where we switch to the A7.'

'The problem is,' Sian said, 'that the boat pulled into Sotogrande fifteen minutes ago. And it was met by — '

'A black Mercedes.' I nodded. 'Skaill. In that monster he'll leave us for dead.'

'Also,' Sian said, 'you were right. There was a woman with Skaill's two men. But Eleanor's not only tough, she's also got common sense. She's decided struggling is a waste of time; the three of them looked so companionable they could have been out for that evening stroll you were talking about.'

* * *

Romero came through on the phone with Skaill's address when, shortly after Rio Verde,

234

I'd switched to the Autovia del Mediterráneo, had negotiated the clover leaf above Marbella that took me onto the A355 and was heading north through Huerta del Prado towards Ojén.

'Villa Conquistador,' Sian said, managing to suppress a giggle. 'That's what Skaill's called his ex-pat residence. It's off Calle de Nacimiento.'

Calum raised a questioning eyebrow.

'Depending on the context, Calle can mean street, road, lane, path — whatever.' She'd dug a road map out of one of the Land Rover's pockets, and it rustled crisply as she opened it wide, then folded it into a neat square. 'Anyway, according to this, Calle de Nacimiento curls off the top of the town of Ojén like a stray wisp of hair, and that's where Skaill lives. Somewhere. We'll have to look for the name.'

'In the dark?'

'If you don't put your foot down, yes.'

The sun had dropped below the horizon, and the shadows had softened. For a while the countryside was barren, ochre dirt and sparse scrub. Then, as we drove further into the hills, there was more greenery on top of the rocky outcrops around which the road swooped and curved, and in the middle distance timbered crags and peaks soared into the evening skies.

'I know you haven't been dwelling on it,' Sian said quietly, 'but as far as we know it was Skaill who murdered Tim. Or had him murdered.'

'Believe me, it's constantly in my mind. Priority is getting Eleanor out of his clutches, but I'm certainly going to have it out with him. And if he doesn't come up with a story that I can believe, Ronnie Skaill is going back with us to face the music.'

'There's nothing that man can say that any of us should believe,' Calum said. 'And if you don't take him back to Gib for your brother's murder, I'll make damn sure he goes back anyway for the kidnap of your mother.'

'I'm touched,' I said.

'Isn't that a euphemism for crazy?'

'Well, crazy or not,' Sian said, 'right now it's make your mind up time. As in, how are the three of us going to handle this when we reach the villa?'

'A difficult one to answer,' I said, 'when we've no idea what we're going to encounter.'

'Let's assume the worst. We were hoping the place would be empty, but that's all changed. Skaill should get there before us. We know he's got two of his thugs, and there'll be enough weapons to cut us to ribbons.'

'If we knock on the door and walk in to

face two big bastards with Kalashnikovs, we won't have a single bargaining chip between us,' Calum said.

'I've got one,' I said, listening to worn tyres squeal as I took a tight bend too fast. Sian's head clonked against the window. She glared at me, rubbed her scalp then fiddled with the rubber band holding her pony-tail.

'It had better be good,' she said, elastic between her teeth as she twirled her hair round a forefinger.

'It'll frighten Skaill to death, make grown men tremble. Effect the release of one kidnap victim, and we'll leave in triumph to the sound of distant trumpets.'

Calum grinned. 'I remember the book. Seems to me it was something to do with cavalry which, as we're in southern Spain, I don't think we should rely on.'

'Look under your feet.'

He bent, hit the front seat with his head as I braked for another bend, then rocked back as I touched the accelerator. When he straightened, he was holding a long object wrapped in a dirty blanket.

Sian was peering over the squab, watching him. I heard her gasp.

'Well, well,' Calum said. 'If the cavalry aren't available, then I suppose this will have to do.'

'How in God's name,' Sian said, 'did you manage that? I know Tim had it, but Romero was there on the boat.'

'It was down the back of the cushion Tim was lying on,' I said. A quick glance in the mirror showed me Calum running a finger along the engraving on the shotgun's barrel that had been worn smooth with use. 'If you remember, I asked Romero for a moment alone with my dead brother.'

'Yes, but how did you get it out, where did you hide it?'

'I reached up and fed it down my shirt so that it lay along my spine with the muzzle down my jeans. When leaving I slung my jacket nonchalantly over my shoulder so it covered the bulge of the stock.'

Calum was again poking about by his feet. He raised a hand, waggled a small, battered oblong carton so I could see it in the mirror.

'I won't even ask you where you put this box of cartridges.'

'Strangely enough, they were here in the Land Rover. Previous owners must have left them and, yes, I've checked and they fit.'

'So is it loaded?'

'Yep.'

'Christ, and I'm waggling it about like a bloody baton. Any Highland ghillie will tell you you're supposed to leave these weapons

238

broken when loaded — '

'I think we're getting close.'

Sian had been concentrating on the road in case I drove us all into a ditch, or worse. She'd spotted the sign for Ojén. She pointed. I indicated, pulled off the A-355 and swooped onto another road that was narrower but still good.

'Looks promising. How far, and how do I get to Villa Conquistador?'

'Don't get your hopes up. There's some way to go yet. This road wriggles about like a snake in its death throes. When it gets to Ojén it bisects the town horizontally and heads north-east. To get to Calle de Nacimiento we've got to go north-west, which means we have to leave this road and cut through the top half of the town.' She was moving her finger across the map, and shaking her head. 'I say 'cut' which suggests a nice clean line; in reality, it's a maze. With the distance still to go on this road, and then all those narrow Spanish streets to negotiate, I reckon it'll take us another . . . oh . . . half-hour?'

I managed it in twenty minutes. By that time night was falling, but we had no difficulty finding Villa Conquistador because Ronnie Skaill had erected a big ranch-style name-board across the entrance to a long drive. And when we'd traversed that, with all the Land Rover's lights off to make our approach as covert as possible, it was to find the place deserted. The house — which was exactly as Sian had visualized it — was in darkness.

For some reason, despite picking up his men and their captive at Sotogrande a good twenty minutes ahead of us and travelling the rest of the way in a powerful car that could leave the Land Rover wallowing in its wake, Ronnie Skaill was somewhere behind us. Against all the odds, we'd beaten him to it.

# 22

'There can be only one explanation,' Calum said. 'He's not going to hold Eleanor in the villa. He must have another place, either here in Ojén, or somewhere in Marbella.'

We were still sitting in the Land Rover. I'd pulled around the side of the house so that if Skaill did return unexpectedly we'd be out of sight.

The front forecourt was an expanse of coloured gravel with curving ornamental walls and plants in stone and terracotta pots of various sizes grouped around tall palms. From where I'd parked we were looking across a rear terrace with a stone balustrade that stretched the length of the house. Below that there was a landscaped rockery, and a curved flight of white marble steps leading down to the pool. The rear of the house faced south, and beyond the gardens and pool, in the far distance, we could see the twinkling lights of Marbella and the warm memory of the sun lingering on the flat waters of the Mediterranean.

It was a scene of sub-tropical tranquillity, but because we knew it was an oasis built by a rich crook, over it all there hung an air of tawdriness, and of menace. That menace was intensified by the situation.

Romero had rubbished the idea of a JFK style killing in the narrow streets of Gibraltar, but the rough scrub here to the north of Ojén was ideal terrain. Eleanor's abduction had lured us to Ojén, the darkened house could be a trap. We could sit there all night, or we could venture out of the Land Rover. Skaill knew exactly what we would do. Waiting was not an option. If he had positioned his sniper, Georgia, a couple of hundred yards away on higher ground, with a 'scoped rifle . . .

'Doesn't matter if he's planning on holding her in an apartment or a scruffy wee shed,' Calum said after a while. 'If it was me I'd make sure Eleanor was secure, maybe tied and gagged if she was still acting stroppy, then come back up here to make a phone call in comfort. To you.'

'Well of course it'd be to me, it doesn't need a clairvoyant to work that out — '

'Jack,' Sian said, a soothing note in her voice.

'Yes, all right, I know, it's time for steady nerves and clear heads.' I took a deep breath. 'OK, Calum, let's say you're right. Skaill had two men with him when he came to the bungalow. He's probably used the same two today — '

'They were on the boat,' Sian said.

'Yes, and he's going to leave one or both of them with Eleanor.'

'One,' Sian said. 'He's a coward, he'll make sure he's got a bodyguard.'

'That man will be armed. What about Skaill?'

'Probably not,' Calum said. 'He lets others do his dirty work, and won't want to be caught carrying.'

I nodded absently, still worried about a trap.

'You don't think this is suspicious? House in darkness. An open invitation. You said there was only one explanation, but I can think of another.'

'So can I,' Calum said, 'but I was keeping quiet because of your fragile nerves. If there is a man out there with a rifle, there's no way we can know.'

'Until we step out of the Land Rover.'

'But that's a chance we have to take, if we're going to finish this.' Calum grinned. 'Or you've got to take; the bullet will have your name on it.'

'In the darkness,' I said, 'he'll take out both of us to make sure.'

'Ah, but you're getting out first, pal. If you go down, we're out of here.'

'Really, Calum,' Sian said, 'I do admire the

way you think of everything.'

'Yes, all right,' I said, 'so we look on the bright side. I step out. There is no sniper. Calum breaks into the house. Once inside, we've got the advantage, the element of surprise.'

'And the shiny shotgun,' Sian said.

'Against the kind of dinky little pistol the bodyguard'll be carrying — '

'Or AK-47.'

' — we can't lose. Come on, let's do it.'

★   ★   ★

Skaill must have left in a hurry. But had he set the alarms? There was only one way we could find out. Calum found a stone of the right size in the landscaped rockery, and used it to smash through the patio doors into the conservatory. His impressive housebreaking skills. Very subtle. When the glass had stopped tinkling the silence was so intense I could hear Sian's soft breathing, my pulse hissing in my ears. An animal, frightened by the noise, crashed away through the bushes.

The alarm had not been activated. No siren howled. No security lights turned night into day.

Calum poked a hand through the shattered glass, found the catch, and we were in.

The conservatory had the normal quota of wicker chairs with thick cushions dimpled with buttons, big flowering plants in heavy stone pots, an atmosphere as damp and humid as a sealed greenhouse. The inner glass doors were misted with condensation, but not locked. They slid open to allow access to a huge living room with a tiled floor, scattered Persian rugs, heavy marble occasional tables that I thought had gone out of fashion. A 54-inch plasma TV hung like a blank painting on one wall. There was the heavy scent of pot-pourri, and enough light from outside for us to move easily without tripping over the furniture or knocking over the tall lamps. Sian scooted through the interior door and her footsteps pattered hither and yon as she quickly searched the rest of the house. She reported back, a little breathless, to state the obvious: there was nobody at home.

'So what have we got?' I said. My pulse was hammering. Tension was making my voice squeak. 'This room, a hall leading to the front door . . . ?'

'The front door's glazed, so we stay clear of that,' Sian said, nodding. 'The kitchen's alongside this room, windows overlooking the terrace and pool, another two sitting-rooms overlooking the forecourt and drive. I think there's a connecting door leading to a single-storey annexe. Probably a gym, maybe an indoor pool.'

'Forget everything except where we are now, the hall, and the front door,' Calum said. 'What about phones?'

'I didn't see one in the hall.'

'There's a cordless over there.' I pointed to one of the marble tables. 'Bound to be others upstairs, especially if he's got an office.'

'Check the front rooms,' Calum said, and again Sian scooted away.

'Nothing,' she said when she returned. 'And I guarantee he won't go upstairs. Long drive, nerves shot. He'll come in here, get the bodyguard to pour him a strong drink' — she indicated the naff bamboo-fronted mini-bar in the corner — 'then use that phone.'

'Last thing,' Calum said, 'will they be able to see the Land Rover?'

'I'll move it further round,' Sian said, and she darted out through the conservatory.

Calum grinned. His eyes were dancing, sparkling in the gloom.

'Plan A is . . . ?'

'A key turns in the lock. The front door opens. We let them come in. You're upstairs, lurking — '

'Lurking?'

'Your speciality. Ready to pounce if I'm in

trouble. Sian is — '

'Over here, by the conservatory,' Sian said, coming back in. 'A stunning distraction, a vision in jeans and cotton blouse silhouetted against luminous night skies.'

'You were too quick out there.'

'Stop worrying. I checked. They won't see it, it's fine where it is.'

'So I'm lurking,' Calum said, 'and Sian's distracted — '

'Distracting,' Sian said. 'Drawing their eyes to me in disbelief as they walk into the room. Holding their attention for those first vital moments.'

'While I, waiting by the door,' I said, 'step out while they're still gobsmacked and jam the shotgun muzzle into Skaill's shell-like.'

'Crude, but oh so bloody effective,' Calum said, giving me an admiring glance. 'And plan B.'

'With a perfect plan A, who needs a fall back?'

'You'd better be right, because you're out of thinking time,' Sian said. 'When I was out checking the Land Rover, headlights on the Calle de Nacimiento were rapidly approaching the entrance to Villa Conquistador.'

'Linguistically she cannot be faulted,' Calum said. 'The words just roll off her tongue, whereas admiration leaves me speechless.'

'Yes, well, if you've quite finished that'll be the Inca advance guard we can hear,' I said. 'Take up your positions.'

★  ★  ★

I could hear the overhead floorboards creaking like geriatric knees as Calum settled at the top of the stairs. For a weapon, he'd taken a shiny 9-iron from the leather golf bag standing by the front door. He reckons the head's heavier than a sand-iron's, while a driver's got a snappy, flexible shaft but is too awkward for close combat.

Sian had switched on one of the low table lamps. It had a dusky golden shade, and that, combined with a low wattage bulb, created the intimate lighting she needed for her seductive pose to smite Skaill most effectively.

I had pushed the door to and was standing so that I would be behind it when it opened. A doorstop shaped like a tiny dragon was set into the floor. If the door hit that there'd be just enough room between door and wall for me and the shotgun.

Gravel's damn near as good as a guard dog. It crunched like breaking ice as the car swung onto the forecourt. Headlights swept across the glazed front door and lit up the hall. Then they went out, doors slammed, and there was more gravel crunching as two people approached the house.

A key turned in the lock. The door swung open with a faint creak of hinges, and even from where I was standing I could feel the breath of cooler air.

Skaill noticed something else. He must have been part bloodhound.

'Someone's been in here.'

'Been in here, or is in here still?'

The second voice had an American accent. That made him the bigger of the two thugs: Georgia, the southern sniper.

'I don't know,' Skaill said. 'But I've got a nose for these things. Somebody invades your premises, you can detect 'em by smell — don't you find that?'

'Not unless it's a family of skunks.'

'Yeah, you're right. Maybe Paquita sprayed her under arms with cologne before she knocked off.'

From my position, I could see nothing. I could hear the soft whisper of sandals on tiles. While talking, the two men were moving slowly along the hall. Skaill would still be suspicious. I knew he and the other man, Georgia, were talking for effect. Skaill would have nudged the big man, gestured, mouthed silent words of warning. Georgia would have nodded and reached under his arm. The pistol he carried there in a holster would now be in his hand. And I knew Skaill would send him in first.

I looked across at Sian. She was standing leaning against the glass doors, as if caught gazing across the terrace. One hand was down by her side, lightly holding against her thigh a fold of the gold floor-length curtains that were draped behind her. She'd undone the three top buttons of her blouse. Interior swellings were urging it open. The pony-tail had gone. Hair like burnished gold brushed her shoulders. Against the night skies it outshone the dusky glow from the table lamp.

I rolled my eyes and put a hand to my heart. She stuck out her tongue.

Then a foot hit the door, hard. It flew open. I'd flattened myself against the wall. Now I screwed up my face in anticipation of disaster. But the door hit the dragon and rebounded. There was a slap as it was stopped by someone's palm.

'Well, well, would you look at this.'

Georgia. He came all the way into the room. Skaill moved up alongside him. He was closest to the door; it was his palm the door had hit. They were both staring across at Sian. She'd half-turned towards them, as if startled by the intrusion. Her blue eyes were wide. We'd gambled that in the dim light and with her hair loose neither of them would instantly recognize her for the woman they had seen in Eleanor's bungalow. Not instantly. But the penny didn't take long to drop.

'Hang on,' Skaill said, 'that's Scott's bird and if she's here — '

He stopped abruptly as his jaws clamped shut. I'd poked the cool double rings of the shotgun's barrels hard into his right ear.

As I did so, there was a glitter of whirling metal and a sickening crunch. Without a sound, Georgia crumpled to the floor. The pistol fell from his hand, slid across the tiles and skittered to a stop on one of the scattered rugs.

'Damn it,' Calum Wick said, 'I'm in the bunker.'

# 23

Georgia was sitting on the floor against the wall. His knees were drawn up, his forearms resting on them, hands hanging loose. Blood trickled from his scalp to his ear and dripped onto his shoulder. His eyes were hooded, the look in them ugly.

Calum was standing over him, but not too close. The big American's pistol dangled loose in his hand.

'Funny name, that,' Calum said casually, 'for a man.'

'John Wayne was really Marion,' I said.

'And Johnny Cash sang about a boy named Sue,' Sian said.

Only seconds had passed since the two men had walked into the room. Calum had downed Georgia with an immaculate swing. I'd pushed Skaill flat onto one of the settees so it would be impossible for him to get up quickly, then backed away with the shotgun at the ready. The curtain was still swaying to stillness behind Sian as she came across the room, fastening buttons.

Skaill had said nothing. I couldn't fathom the look on his face, in his eyes. The emotion

I saw there wasn't strong enough for fear. I could understand nerves, the jitters, but this was something else. What I saw there wasn't even close to what a man in his position should be feeling.

Then Sian made a sudden rush for the door.

'Jack,' she cried, 'someone's moving the car.'

'Watch these two, Calum.'

I charged out after her. Already she'd flung open the front door. I reached her, grabbed her arm.

'Careful.'

'We've both done this many times, Jack.'

'In uniform, with weapons and backup.'

'These are untrained, out of condition, third-rate thugs.'

We were talking in low tones while hanging back, listening. I could hear the car: the soft purr of an engine at idling speed. It was going nowhere in a hurry. Shotgun held high across my chest I slipped outside, my shirt rasping against the white stucco wall.

Following me, her hand on my shoulder, Sian said, 'It's pulled over. It's parking outside the annexe.'

'Yes. That'll be the second goon, Cazza. But there's another man there we hadn't calculated — '

'No! It's not a man. Jack, Eleanor's in the car.'

As she spoke I saw through the rear window the loose, familiar white hair, and within me hope flared. They'd brought her here. To me. Elation made my head swim. Then common sense kicked in. I could almost reach out and touch her — but she was as far away as ever. A beautiful, fragile bargaining chip. No wonder Skaill was displaying mixed emotions.

'He'll be armed,' Sian said, as the car stopped and the driver's door clicked open.

'But so far he doesn't know we're here.'

'He'll stay close to her anyway. If you fire that shotgun there'll be a lot of that collateral damage.'

She didn't finish. Thinking while talking, she'd reached a decision and was off. She ran at a crouch straight across the gravel, making for one of the low walls.

The Mercedes was away to the right, standing with its boot towards us. The big thug, Cazza, was already out of the car. He opened the rear door and dragged Eleanor out by her arm. I heard her cry out in pain. She struggled, tried to shake him off. He swung her bodily to face the annexe. Her legs buckled. Clinging to each other like drunks, they stumbled away from the Mercedes.

Then Cazza heard the crunch of Sian's feet on the gravel.

He pushed Eleanor hard. Her back hit the door of the annexe. She slid down slowly, clutching her head. Now it was anger in me that flared out of control. I stepped away from the wall, lifted the shotgun.

'Get away from her and put your hands up,' I roared.

With a lunge, he ran for the Mercedes. I tracked him with the shotgun. The foresight was pinned on his broad back. He hit the bonnet with the flat of his hands and took off. Eleanor was still huddled against the heavy door, out of the line of fire. I pulled the trigger. The side window blew out in a shower of sparkling fragments. But Cazza had vaulted to safety. He slid, dropped in front of the radiator. Glass shone like rain in his black hair. He ducked down, and I caught the glint of a weapon in his hand.

'Hold it there,' Sian called. Like Cazza, she'd vaulted into cover and was behind the ornamental wall. 'There's a shotgun one side of you, and I've got you covered. A cross-fire, get it?'

His reply was a bullet. He'd fired at Sian. There was a crack, the shrill whine of a ricochet. Stone splinters hissed angrily.

On the still night air my unarmed Soldier

Blue's deliberate laugh mocked his impotence.

I began walking towards the Mercedes, keeping its bulk between me and the gunman. The shotgun made me ten feet tall, but only one barrel was loaded. Spare cartridges were in the Land Rover — halfway round the house. But how much fire power did I need for one man with a popgun?

'Georgia's out of it with concussion,' I called, inching forward. 'He carelessly put his head in the way of a swinging golf club. And Ronnie . . . '

I could see the top of Sian's head. Her blonde hair was a moving flame in the gloom. She worked her way along the other side of the wall. It bordered a shrubbery. She was creeping silently across soft earth. The wall curved gently towards the annexe's far wall. At its closest point it would put her no more than six feet away from Cazza — and she would be behind him.

Eleanor was also watching her. She was still in her gardening clothes: trousers, a green smock and floppy cotton sun hat. Now sitting with her back against the annexe door, she had a ringside seat and could see all three of us. The faint light of a rising moon was reflected in her eyes as she looked across at me.

'Yeah,' Cazza said, 'what about Ronnie?'

He was listening to me. Probably calculating his chances. Wondering if Skaill was paying him enough to go up against a weapon that had ruined a fine Mercedes. I hoped that meant he wasn't keeping a watchful eye on Sian.

'My colleague in there is covering him with Georgia's gun. That means you'll get no help from your boss. You're on your own. Last man standing.'

'Last man standing wins. If that's me, you'd better put down that shotgun.'

'You? Christ, you're putting a lot of faith in that tiny pistol — '

'It's big enough to blow a big hole in your white-haired old mother if you don't back off.'

'Ignore him, Jack. He's bluffin'. He's already had a taste of my claws, and I'm tellin' him now if he goes after you or Sian I'll be on him like a tiger.'

The brave words rang out, the Liverpool accent thickened by emotions that didn't include fear.

'You're up against three of us,' I said, moving closer, 'and I've got a good idea who scares you the most so it's up to you, last man standing, or first man dying — '

I broke off. There was a sudden loud crash

from the main house and a voice roared in rage or pain. At the same time, two shots rang out. The noise panicked Cazza. He forgot caution and began to stand up to see what was going on. And as wood splintered and there was the sound of shattering glass that was probably the mini-bar and its bottles and glasses toppling to the tiled floor, Sian came over the wall like an Olympic hurdler and launched herself at Cazza's back.

Her weight plus momentum slammed his shins and thighs hard against the car's radiator grille. He grunted in pain. Holding him there with her legs braced she clamped her left forearm across his throat, hooked that hand in her right elbow and curled her right hand around the back of his head. The classic choke hold. His eyes widened with shock. His free hand plucked futilely at her arm. He straightened to his full height, lifted her onto her toes, then off the ground, but by then I was coming around the car.

His face was turning purple. Through bulging eyes he saw me coming. He raised the pistol. I swiped it out of his hand with the shotgun, a cricketer executing a perfect drive to mid-on, then whipped the gun around in a backhand swing and knocked him out with a blow to the temple.

# 24

'There's a blank space on your wall, and a hook with nothing hanging on it,' I said. 'The size looks about right. I take it you haven't recovered your Dutch masterpiece — or is it that you got it back but what with the nuisance of kidnapping and everything you haven't had time to hang it?'

'I haven't got it,' Ronnie Skaill said through clenched teeth.

'And, talking of hanging — did you murder my brother?'

He was white-faced and sweating, a tired old man stripped to the waist on the settee as Sian, with Eleanor's help, dressed the gunshot wound in the fleshy part of his shoulder. Georgia was lying on one of the scattered rugs in the recovery position, unconscious, breathing in a bubbly way through his mouth. Cazza had been helped unsteadily into the house and was sprawled, somewhat dazed, definitely bewildered, on a chair in the conservatory. The bruise on his temple was swollen and shiny in the moonlight.

Calum, unfazed, was toying with the

259

number 9 iron. Georgia's pistol jutted from his hip pocket. The room reminded me of those I'd seen after Australian cyclones have blown through.

'I'm not a killer,' Skaill said wearily.

'Oh. What about Haggard?'

'Gomez has seen Romero. He has told him Haggard's death had nothing to do with me.'

'Gomez, your son's defence counsel?'

'Yeah, yeah.'

'The man he will now rely on because you're no longer in a position to help him.' I held his gaze. 'Haggard's death may have had nothing to do with you,' I said, 'but you must know who was involved.'

'Must I?'

'And whoever was involved must have provided the bloodstained leather jacket.'

Skaill's head shot up. He winced, reached across to stay Sian's ministering hand for a moment as he closed his eyes. When he opened them again he was looking at me with such intensity that I knew his mind was racing, replaying old scenes, recoiling from inevitable conclusions.

'What leather jacket?'

'When Haggard was dumped he was wearing a leather jacket — '

'Christ, how many times d'you need telling? *I never saw Haggard*. Got it? I was

260

offered a way to keep Nick out of jail, and I fuckin' jumped at it. This guy knew the fairground killer, knew where he was in Gib. If I put this to you, told you he was yours on condition — oh, hell, why go on, you know the rest — '

'The leather jacket Haggard was wearing was the one worn by the fairground killer.'

'So what? This guy I was dealin' with knew him, I told you that. He must have got the jacket off him, put it on Haggard . . . ' He trailed off, realizing how weak it sounded. 'Anyway, how'd you know it was the killer's jacket, how can that be *proved?*'

'It was stained with blood. You're no fool. You must have heard of DNA. The blood was a match for Tommy Mack's, and for Amanda's.'

Then Calum chipped in.

'Time to make phone calls, Jack,' he said. 'Yon big fellow on the mat's not looking too healthy. And if Skaill here didn't kill young Tim, Romero should be informed.'

So, for the moment, we left it at that.

I located numbers in a book Skaill provided, told the Marbella police that wounded men involved in kidnapping a woman in Gibraltar were tied up at the Villa Conquistador in Ojén, and that an ambulance was needed.

261

The helicopter had returned to La Linea, and Romero was back in Gibraltar. I caught him on his mobile. He was at the Royal Gibraltar police headquarters at New Mole House on Rosia Road, and my news only confirmed what he already knew. While he was in the air watching *El Pajaro Negro* sail into Sotogrande, his men had been down to Marina Bay, talked to Roland Girard and searched the gin palace. They had found a malacca cane, a painting, and another pistol. Girard had talked. He was under arrest for theft, and the murder of Tim Scott.

And so, when Ronnie Skaill was cleanly bandaged and bundled back into his clothing, we bound the two thugs with plastic line cut from a clothes airer, and leaving them comfortable in the conservatory with the house doors open and all lights blazing, five of us scrambled into the Land Rover and we headed back to Gibraltar.

I sat in the back with Sian and Eleanor. Calum took the wheel. He drove fast and with great skill, leaving me to concentrate on the questions I was going to put to Ronnie Skaill. We had achieved what we had set out to do in Marbella, which was free Eleanor, but we had little else to show for the long drive. Romero was dealing with Tim's killer. Harry Haggard's death was a tragedy, but not our concern. I was determined to clear Tim's name, and that meant finding the man who had murdered Tommy Mack and Amanda Skaill.

The man I was convinced had all the answers was sitting in the passenger seat next to Calum.

# 25

'You know you're going to serve time for kidnapping, don't you?'

'Knackers. It's my word against hers.' Skaill jerked a thumb over his shoulder. 'Alzheimers has kicked in; she's lost her marbles; lucid Lily she is not.'

I glanced across Sian at Eleanor. My mother winked at me, unperturbed.

'Where's Terry?'

'Terry? In the UK. What the fuck d'you want with him?'

'He was there recently, wasn't he? You sent him. You were anxious to know how the investigation into the fairground murders was getting on.'

'I sent him nowhere. Why should I? Amanda was dead, your kid brother was goin' down for murder. The fairground killin's were of no interest.'

'So you didn't send him?'

'I told you.'

'Then who did? Think about it. Who'd have reason to worry?'

'You would.' He half turned, grinning.

'You're absolutely right, but it's not the

answer I was looking for.' I thought for a minute. 'Terry was on the same flight as me, returning to Gib. So was Harry Haggard. Haggard had his own ideas about the fairground murders. But when he arrived in Gib he was picked up by two men in a black Mercedes. That was the last time he was seen alive. Which suggests Terry knows a lot about that particular killing.'

'Why? What's the connection?' He was turning in his seat now, leaning against the door as he stared at me.

'In Haggard's opinion, Tim wasn't guilty.'

'You think that about Terry because you don't know him. But you're wrong. He's a good lad. Persil. Squeaky clean.'

'Unlike Nick.'

'Yeah, well . . . '

'All right, let's talk about Nick, because there's nothing stopping me testifying now. Tell me, Skaill, just supposing I am right and Nick did shoot that bent copper, Bobby Greenoak — why did he do it?'

'He didn't.'

'No, hang on, play along with me for a minute. I'm supposing. It's purely hypothetical. Nick pulled a gun, and shot Greenoak dead. Hypothetically. Why?'

We'd dipped down from the main road from Ojén and were speeding back along the

Mediterranean coast. Calum was looking straight ahead, driving with one hand on the wheel. Sian had her head against my shoulder, but I knew she was awake, and listening. Eleanor was asleep.

Skaill drummed his fingers on the squab, still half turned but gazing ahead through the windscreen.

Without taking his eyes from the road, he said, 'He slagged off my family. Nick's family.'

'Did he now? Mentioned the unmentionable?'

I waited a moment, then said, 'Have you ever wondered why Amanda was murdered?'

'No.'

'If that slagging off had something to do with her, with Amanda — would that be a reason?'

Now he looked at me. His eyes were blank, but he was breathing faster than normal. The hand on the squab was clenched, the knuckles white.

'Why don't you tell me?' he said softly. 'Tell me what you're getting at.'

'If Greenoak knew something, he must have got it from somewhere. Calum spoke to . . . a woman in the UK who had a nasty tale to tell.'

'Fuckin' rumours,' Skaill said, fury in his voice. He shook his head, dragged in a breath.

'You've heard them?'

266

'I know what Greenoak said. Nick told me, he was devastated.'

'And Greenoak paid for it.'

'He was wrong anyway. Greenoak was. I don't know where he heard it, but what he was suggestin' never happened.'

'Suppose it did happen.'

'No, it didn't.'

'Hypothetically again. Worst case scenario. Suppose it did happen. Had been happening for some time. Not you — '

'Damn right, not me.'

'But . . . someone. And Amanda couldn't take any more. She was going to tell. Name names.'

'She wouldn't go to the social, the police.'

'But she'd go to you. And you have a reputation. If she gave you a name . . . '

Skaill turned away. He dragged out a handkerchief and mopped his brow. The smell of sweat was strong in the Land Rover.

'So we're back to Haggard again,' I said. 'Just as we were in your villa. Same dead man, same questions. Who set up that business with his dead body, Skaill? Haggard's body? Who told you he could deliver the fairground killer?'

Silence. Skaill's shoulders were stiff with tension. I could see the muscles in his jaw working.

'One of your men. Isn't that what you said when you came to see us in the bungalow? Or was it me telling you? I think it was, because I'd heard it from my contacts in Liverpool, and I passed it on to you. Doesn't matter anyway. Body provided, it had to be one of your men. One of your men, the fairground killer. Proof? Well, we've already talked about this. He as good as convicted himself, because he dressed Harry Haggard up in a leather jacket stained with your daughter's blood.'

'Jesus Christ,' Ronnie Skaill whispered.

'Mm,' I said. 'Absolutely. You know who it is, because he came to you. Now, what are you going to do about it?'

★ ★ ★

He didn't tell us, of course. All the way back along that coast road with the moon painting white light on the endless miles of concrete and tarmac, picking out glossy palm fronds swaying in the warm breeze, washing clean the white houses with tiled roofs and, far across the inky Mediterranean and its wide sweeping bays, the water catchments on the eastern slopes of the massive, brooding shape of the Rock of Gibraltar; all that way, then further, along the streets of La Linea de la

268

Concepción and through the border crossing where the guards looked at him, recognized him, yet of course asked for his passport — he kept his mouth firmly closed.

Once through and driving into Gibraltar, I demanded his passport. He handed it over, and at that moment I should have realized something was seriously wrong. Perhaps I did. But what I didn't do was try to work out what it was, so that when, close to Casemates, he waited for Calum to slow down for a bend then simply opened the passenger door and stepped out, I was caught napping.

'Oh my God,' Eleanor said softly.

'Leave him,' Calum said, not stopping. 'He can't harm us now.'

'Damn it,' I swore, watching Skaill dart across the pavement and move out of sight down a gap between the high-rise buildings.

'He's gone.'

'But not far,' Sian said, straightening and yawning. 'You've got his passport, his boat's in Sotogrande.'

'Do you not feel,' Calum said, picking up speed again and swinging onto Queensway, 'that what's happened just now was inevitable?'

'In what way?'

'Once handed over to Romero he would be in custody, his freedom gone. It's possible that lawyer Gomez will get him out on bail, but probably not until the morning. And Ronnie Skaill has things to do.'

'Mm. He has an abuser, a killer to confront.'

'And we've all got a fair idea who that is, haven't we?' Sian said. 'Skaill must have known for some time, but he wouldn't admit it even to himself. I was watching him when you told him about the leather jacket. I thought he was going to be sick.'

Calum was swinging into Ragged Staff Road as I dug out my mobile phone. DI Luis Romero answered at once. I told him briefly what had happened: Eleanor safe, Ronnie Skaill back in Gibraltar but on the loose with no passport, nowhere to go.

'Then he will go to his apartment, where Nick is staying,' Romero said.

'Maybe. But, anyway, I suggest you get a police car down there without delay.'

'I would do that, of course, without your prompting, but you make it sound . . . what . . . a matter of life and death? I do not understand what is going on, what it is you are not telling me.'

'And it's too involved to tell you now, Luis, it would take too long. You've got that car to dispatch, and I want to get Eleanor home. Just to reassure you: the only people likely to be in danger are those close to Ronnie Skaill. Closest.'

'And that is reassurance?'

'Meant to be. Anyway, just one more thing: if Ronnie's not there, talk to Nick. Tell him what's been happening. About the citizen's arrest of his father. Also, make sure he knows that on the way back from the villa his father and I had a frank talk.'

'Do you want me to tell him what that conversation was about?'

'No. I want him to stew.'

'Stew?'

'Think long and hard through the night's dark hours. Worry himself sick.'

'And you are not giving me a hint, a clue?'

'You're a detective, Luis. Work it out.'

'Perhaps I am not as clever as you. Or is it that I do not have all the information? Do not know if your talk with Skaill was about fairground murders, the murder of a bent copper, a DS from England — '

'Or all three of those.'

He chuckled. 'That is beyond clever, it is confusing. Take your mother home, Jack. I will call you when, one way or another, the minor matter of Ronnie Skaill's whereabouts is resolved.'

\*　\*　\*

Reg was at the bungalow door when we drove up, the warm light from the lamp outlining his lean frame and turning grey hair into a halo of pink candy-floss. It was close to midnight. When the Land Rover was safely off the road and we'd all piled into the living room, he gave Eleanor a hug strong enough to break bones. His eyes, as he looked over her shoulder at me, were brimming with tears. Then, as she looked back at me and rolled her eyes heavenwards, he took her hand in his and led her through to the bedroom. He didn't emerge until, comfortable in a soft nightdress decorated with pink roses and with her hair tied back with a dusky ribbon, she was sitting propped against plumped-up pillows waiting for her Horlicks.

Sian was stretched out on the *chaise-longue* with her hands laced behind her blonde head, looking fit enough to break wild ponies. Calum was at the window, probably reflecting on the highly original uses to which he could now put a number nine golf club. I joined Reg in the kitchen. When he'd departed with two steaming mugs of Horlicks and a plate of chocolate digestive biscuits, I boiled a kettle, poured water on three mugs of instant coffee, debated for probably half a second then thought to hell with it and added splashes of brandy generous enough to sedate elephants.

When I returned, laden, to the living room, my mind had been busy and I'd reached the conclusion that Sian's remark after Skaill bolted from the Land Rover was some way off the truth.

'We're assuming that when Skaill jumped out of the Land Rover he'd gone after a killer, aren't we?'

'I think so,' Sian said. 'A killer who has also been abusing Ronnie's daughter.'

'Yes,' I said, handing out the drinks, 'but do we really know who that man is?'

Sian frowned. 'Isn't there amongst us something like an unspoken consensus?'

'I don't know — is there?'

'Well if there's not,' Calum said, 'we'll have to go through it one laborious step at a time. Starting with Bobby Greenoak, the first person to die. According to Ronnie, it was Greenoak who made the awful suggestion of naughty fumblings and gropings and God knows what else in the Skaill family. If true, then that accusation led directly to the other murders.'

Sipping my drink, I couldn't fault his reasoning.

'And because I saw Nick leaving Lagoon Deep with the gun, we can be pretty sure

Nick murdered Greenoak. But apparently Nick then told Ronnie what Greenoak had suggested. That opened a can of worms. From that day on, other members of the family would have been looking over their shoulders. The guilty man would have been terrified, knowing that eventual exposure was inevitable.'

I looked from one to the other, saw thoughtful nods of agreement.

'What we don't know,' I said, 'is if Greenoak named names, or even if he had anything more to go on than ugly rumours.'

'Also,' Sian said, 'as Calum pointed out, it would be interesting to know how that rumour reached Greenoak. A cop in Gibraltar, rumours of mucky goings on in the UK. Where's the connection?'

'There are police officer exchanges, courses, all kinds of things,' I said. 'My guess is he got wind of something going on when he was in the UK — we know the Skaills have got a contact who works with the police — but does it matter?'

'Totally unimportant,' Calum said. 'He found out one way or another, let the cat out of the bag, the news raced through the family like wildfire and in one hell of a wee panic an unknown person flew to the UK and murdered Amanda.'

'Before she could open her mouth and spill the beans, drop him in it,' Sian said. 'For good measure he also cut Tommy Mack's throat and made a reasonable attempt at framing Tim.'

'And while we do know Nick was in the UK at the time of those murders,' I said, 'what we don't know is if Terry Skaill was there at that same time.'

Calum leaned forward, placed his empty mug on the table, sat back with his long legs stretched out and crossed at the ankles. Reg had come through from the bedroom. I guessed Eleanor, exhausted by her ordeal, was fast asleep. Perched on a chair, Reg was hugging a mug of what must have been cold Horlicks.

'I've been overhearing fragments of your discussion,' he said. 'Seems to me the next stage is the death of Harry Haggard.'

'And that,' I said, 'really does bring us to Terry Skaill.'

Sian raised an eyebrow. 'Because?'

'Because as I pointed out to Romero, and to Ronnie, Terry was on the plane with Haggard.' I paused. 'And there's also something else I've just thought of. I'd assumed from the start that Ronnie sent Terry on that trip to the UK to check on the fairground murders investigation. When Ronnie denied doing that on the drive back from Spain, my thinking naturally switched to Nick being behind it. But if *Terry* is the killer, he'd have needed no telling; he would have made the trip to the UK because he'd have been desperate to know if the police were closing in on him.'

'Where that contact you mentioned would have informed him that DS Harry Haggard was openly sceptical of Tim's guilt,' Calum said. 'That put Terry in danger. Action was needed and, lo and behold, Haggard was snatched the very minute he walked out into the Gibraltar sunshine.'

'Mm, and wound up on our doorstep, dead.' I looked at Sian. She was pulling a face, remembering the gruesome details. 'With Harry Haggard,' I said, 'we've reached the last of the murders. Are we any wiser?'

Calum tugged at his beard. 'Do we know if Terry's in Gib?'

'We don't know where he is. All I know for sure is he's got a blonde wife, and lives near Ronnie.'

Sian sighed. 'And although we're pretty sure Nick shot Greenoak — '

She broke off, looking at me. My phone was trilling. It was Romero, phoning from Ronnie Skaill's apartment.

'He is not here, Ronnie Skaill,' the DI said.

'My men are searching, but there is really nowhere for him to hide.'

'And Nick?'

'He is bound by the curfew. He was watching television.'

'You told him his father had been arrested? That he and I had a long talk?'

'Of course.'

'His reaction?'

'A casual shrug of indifference, of who-the-hell-cares. But as he turned away, there was in his eyes emotions there I did not expect to see.'

'Let me guess. He was frightened.'

'In his face and his eyes there was that, plus much more. Shock, despair . . . resignation, perhaps a coming to terms with what he believes is now bound to happen.'

'He knows he'll go down for murder; that would be the resignation, the start of steeling himself for the inevitable. But the fear interests me, because I know that comes from the realization that his father is on the loose and dangerous. I wonder, though,' I said, thinking about what we'd been discussing, 'if that fear was for himself, or for another person?'

'You will have to explain that to me when we have more time,' Romero said. 'Meanwhile . . . '

'Are you going to leave one of your men there, or somewhere close, on the chance that Ronnie Skaill does turn up?'

'That would be logical.'

'Then can I ask you to be illogical?'

'What is the saying? It is more than my job is worth? If Nick Skaill is frightened, then he is frightened of his father. I must give him police protection.' He was silent for a moment. 'What are you expecting to happen, Jack?'

'I'm expecting Ronnie to make his son pay for certain despicable acts he has committed — and I'm not talking about murder, although there's certainly enough of that. The trouble is, he's got two sons and we don't know which one is guilty. I know damn well Ronnie will want the payment to fit the crime, but that's another big problem: we don't know what awful revenge he's got planned, and we've no idea where he intends to carry it out. If you leave Nick exposed, there's just a chance we might find out.'

# 26

## Saturday

Breakfast the next morning was served up by Calum Wick at the sinfully late hour of ten o'clock.

Eight hours earlier I'd rattled the Land Rover down the Rock's upper slopes from Eleanor's bungalow to our apartment in Castle Road. As soon as the door closed behind us Calum had dragged a red Lilo out onto the balcony, and the last we'd seen of him he'd been liberally applying the mosquito repellent. He'd found it in the bathroom cupboard, and it was well out of date. When he woke us the bags under his eyes were touching his bearded cheeks and there were suspicious red blotches everywhere naked skin was visible — and he was stripped to the waist. He'd deliberately laid the breakfast table on the balcony so we could endure some of the same torment. Much to his chagrin, although the sun was already hot enough to trouble basking lizards there were no little humming kamikaze blood suckers patrolling the still air.

Then he told us what had roused him.

'You left your bloody mobile in the Land Rover. What the hell is that haunting ringtone? I thought I was Odysseus listening to the song of the sirens. I almost fell down those damn stone stairs in my haste to be lured, only to discover it was your damn Sony Ericsson. I got there when it was still ringing, but I think there was a snake on the other end. A lot of hissing. Probably having difficulty getting a signal.'

A croissant was suspended on its way to my mouth.

'Who, the snake?'

'Ignore him, Calum,' Sian said, lips rosy from cranberry juice.

I tasted the croissant, chewed pleasurably, sipped coffee.

'So you didn't try to call him back?'

'Snakes don't — '

'Did you?'

'If the caller couldn't reach me,' Calum said, 'then don't you think there would have been the same problem in the reverse direction?'

'So we're none the wiser. What if it was Romero, wanting us to assist?'

'I don't think a bungled citizen's arrest qualifies you, pal.'

A faint melody, dulcet, bewitching, drifted

to us on the warm air.

Sian was looking at me. 'Phone, Jack.'

I looked at Calum. 'Where is it?'

'Where you left it.'

'No. Since I left it, you've used it. Now it's where you left it. Where's that?'

'Same place.'

Sian was shaking her head. 'I'd go and get it,' she said, 'but it's too late. Whoever it was has rung off.'

'Probably another snake,' Calum offered.

Then the apartment's phone rang.

★　★　★

Ronnie Skaill's apartment was in Royal Ocean Plaza, an award-winning high rise block in the new development known as Ocean Village. It was a short stroll along Marina Bay from where *El Pajaro Negro* had been moored. Once again I left the Land Rover where no car should be parked, reminding myself that I really should get one of those printed bits of cardboard I could stick on the dash to tell everyone I was a doctor on call.

I walked through the heat along the edge of flat water that lapped lazily against luxury yachts, smelling the salt of the open sea and the less attractive resinous tang of fibreglass hulls close to blistering. Seagulls ignored me as they strutted, orange beaks lifted haughtily. There was a stillness to the air, a sultry weight and oppressive silence that was the lull before the storm. I knew that from the moment we broke into Skaill's villa and lay in wait for him, events had been heading for a climax that could be explosive, yet the portents I was sensing there on that sweltering marina were more mundane: banks of purple cloud were building in the western skies above the Straits of Gibraltar, and the storm that was approaching was not the climax as linked investigations reached a dénouement — though that would surely come — but a late summer system of fierce squalls that would soon hit the Rock.

Inside the air-conditioned building a lift took me heavenwards, at speed. Skaill's fourteenth-floor apartment door was open. It being now almost eleven o'clock, most of the police who had flocked to the scene — that's if two or three can be called a flock — when their injured colleague was discovered, had long since departed. Luis Romero was at the panoramic window, gazing out over a blue expanse of water where a dozen or more cargo ships were steaming in or out of the bay or waiting at anchor for their turn to enter the harbours of Gibraltar or Algeciras.

282

'How is he?'

Romero turned his head. 'Lacerations. Concussion. He will live to tell me how an experienced police officer could have failed to observe the approach of his attacker.'

'Skaill?'

Romero shrugged.

'And Nick Skaill?'

'No sign of him, or his father.'

'That's worrying.'

'Depends on your viewpoint. Many people would suggest that never seeing them again might be cause for celebration.'

He was still at the window. I joined him. The storm clouds were closing in. Between the rocky coasts of Spain and North Africa, the sea was slate grey. Curtains of rain hung from the swollen clouds like ripped silken petticoats due for a wash.

For a few moments we admired in silence a view that had cost Ronnie Skaill more than half-a-million Gibraltarian quid. I thought of another man who had been in a similar position but was now looking forward to less prestigious accommodation.

'Girard's got one of these, hasn't he?'

'I told you. Same block.'

'But he's not at home?'

Romero smiled. 'Not now, and not for any length of time in the foreseeable future. His luxury apartment will gather dust while he rots.'

'Did he confess?'

'He had no option. We have the gun, his prints are on it, the bullet taken from your brother is a match, and he had the painting that your brother stole from Skaill.'

'And the malacca cane?'

'That too. We will hold it for a while.'

'What about Raven and Pagetti? They had Tim's water-colours.'

'Oh, they delivered OK, in and out like thieves in the night — and, of course, this all happened before your evening of excitement with Ronnie Skaill.'

'And before your man on guard duty went to sleep.'

Romero glowered. 'So, what I'm saying is those paintings were also recovered, and the same now applies: we will hold them, and you will be able to collect in the fullness of time.'

I nodded absently. 'You know,' I said, 'there was a time when I thought there was a link from the dodgy art lover here in Gib to the fairground murders in Liverpool. It's still possible, I suppose, if Girard and Skaill had business connections.'

Romero was shaking his head.

'Enemies, I am sure. The straw leading to your brother's body came from crates containing some of Girard's works of art. He used it in the way he did to try to implicate Skaill.'

Then, as we were interrupted by a sound that was not strident, he looked at me with a raised eyebrow and a sardonic smile.

'Once upon a time,' he said, 'telephone handsets used to look like black dumbbells and sound like old-time police cars racing to an emergency. Now they are flimsy bits of plastic spouting Muzak suitable for a down-market brothel.'

'Excuse me for a moment,' I said, grinning and taking out my mobile as I walked away.

I could hear breathing. It sounded harsh, strained. Also, in the background, seagulls screamed like tormented souls.

'I gave one of my sons a leather jacket for his birthday,' Ronnie Skaill said.

'Congratulations.'

'Isn't it pertinent? Doesn't that tell you all you need to know?'

'Not quite. There's important information missing.'

His chuckle was like someone being strangled.

'Yeah. Like, which son.'

Romero was watching me. I covered the mouthpiece and mouthed 'Calum Wick. Toy soldiers'. His dark eyes registered extreme scepticism.

'You're right,' I said to Skaill. 'Knowing that would put the finishing touches.'

'So here's what you do. You, on your own, no fuckin' cops, come now to the Mediterranean Steps. You know them?'

'Yes. A friend of mine helped construct them.'

'Make it snappy.'

'Consider it done.'

I clicked off, pocketed the phone.

'You do not *construct* toy soldiers,' Romero said softly.

'The shelves on which to stand them,' I said. 'We've got new ones. Calum was impressed.'

'But your toy soldiers are in North Wales.'

'Calum took delivery before he flew out. He's going back soon.'

'Ah.' Romero nodded. 'And all that is true? You wouldn't lie to me, Jack?'

'If I have, it's for a very good reason,' I said, and I turned away and left him to ponder and quietly fume.

# 27

Could I trust Ronnie Skaill? The answer to that was a resounding negative. The trouble was, it was the wrong question. Instead, I should have been asking myself what he was up to; what the hell he was playing at.

So on the drive back to town in the Land Rover, with the first heavy drops of rain spattering the windscreen, I did some mental head scratching, juggled increasingly bizarre possibilities, and eventually settled on the gruesome scenario that seemed to fit Ronnie's frame of mind. He'd lost his daughter, discovered that one of his sons had been abusing her, and wanted me there on the Mediterranean Steps to witness his son's confession. That done, he would kill the lad, and take his own life.

Didn't fit the mentality of an ex-pat crook with nerves of steel and no compassion, a survivor living the life of Reilly on the sun-soaked Spanish coast? Probably not. But unusual events can tear people apart and lead to one explosive act of violence they feel will put things right but is completely out of character — and there I found myself chuckling ironically as my rattling green vehicle climbed Castle Road, because if there was one trait that had always defined Ronnie Skaill's character, it was extreme violence.

On the way up the hill I could see Sian on the apartment's balcony, looking seawards at the rain as she folded the polka-dot parasol and removed it from the table. I tooted the horn. She glanced down, collapsed parasol over her shoulder like a guardsman with rifle at the slope. I flashed the lights in a way I hoped denoted urgency, then pulled in to the kerb and applied the handbrake without switching off the engine. Less than a minute later, she and Calum burst from the building's front door.

'Should have brought capes and sou'westers,' I said, as doors slammed and I pulled away in a cloud of smoke and pointed the Land Rover up the already wet road.

'If we're going fishing,' Calum said, 'this is the wrong direction.'

'You're right about one thing: it is the wrong direction. Skaill phoned. He wants me at the Mediterranean Steps, on my own — and, as you know, Sian, that pathway starts at Jew's Gate and curls precariously around the south and east of the Rock.'

'Precariously,' Calum said.

'As in clinging to the side of the Rock,

sheer drops not for the faint-hearted, fair chance of coming a cropper.'

'Risk of fatal fall increased during stormy weather.'

'Yes, so disregard my remark about capes. In a high wind they'd act like spinnakers.'

Sian was shaking her head. 'So if you two have quite finished letting nerves get the better of you, let me unravel the master plan. When it's done with meandering and clinging to the cliffs, that pathway from Jew's Gate becomes the Med Steps proper and climbs steeply to O'Hara's Battery. You're going to drop us at the top of the Rock. We begin walking down the steep steps from the O'Hara's Battery end. You then race away and proceed along the pathway in the opposite direction, from Jew's Gate.'

'Gingerly,' Calum said.

'With my eyes peeled for ex-pat nutters.'

As the Land Rover carried us higher and we swung around a tight right hand bend that pointed us ever upwards but now heading south, I told them about my brief visit to Royal Ocean Plaza, my talk with Luis Romero, and Skaill's phone call.

'The idea is that if I go to Med Steps, all will be revealed. I'll know which son has been a naughty boy. However, that's just part of it. I think he wants me to witness something

. . . final. A reckoning, if you like.'

'Bear in mind,' Calum said quickly, 'that at least half his troubles can be traced back to your interference.'

'So I could be included in the reckoning? Of course, you're right.'

'But you're hoping that by the time you meet Skaill, your trusty henchmen — '

'Henchpeople.'

'Fellow musketeers,' Sian said, smiling sweetly at me. 'You're hoping we'll be there to save your skin.'

'Should the need arise.'

She nodded. 'And it bloody well will. Ronnie and the guilty son will be trapped in a PI sandwich.'

'And when you're in position,' Calum said, 'he'll put a bullet in his son's skull and watch with a twisted feeling of satisfaction as he tumbles down those rocky slopes.'

Sian was looking at me. 'You agree?'

'I do.'

But, of course, I was wrong.

# 28

By the time I'd brought the Land Rover swooping down Queen's Road and braked to a sideways slithering halt on the small exposed plateau that was Jew's Gate, rain was sweeping almost horizontally across the bay, the wind lifting the seawater into waves that smashed against the distant detached mole. Nature's sheer ferocity was to my advantage. Parking was never allowed anywhere in the area, but in the booth where walkers paid their entrance fee I could see a man with his back to me, his elbows on the desk as he watched the storm through streaming windows.

Skaill's Mercedes was still parked outside his villa to the north of Marbella. He would have brought the guilty son to Jew's Gate by taxi. At gunpoint. So, unnoticed by the fascinated booth attendant, I parked up against the wall and climbed out. I was dressed in T-shirt, jeans and trainers. They were soaked before I had passed through the narrow stone opening with concrete lintel that led to Mediterranean Steps.

For some way the path wound through

dense shrubs, the ground uneven but not tricky. Ahead, the jagged limestone face of the Rock reared into lowering grey skies like an enormous Sphinx eroded by time. The wind was a constant roar. Rain was like a power shower directed at me from behind. I jogged forward with my head down, whipped by flailing wet branches.

I emerged suddenly from the tossing greenery. Ahead, the pathway turned, and dropped abruptly to the right. It was the first stretch of treacherous terrain. The ground was rutted, so hard and dry after the usual long hot summer that it could not absorb the rain. Water was streaming downhill, rushing white-edged rivulets that carried with them yellow mud and loose rocks. I picked my way down gingerly. After some forty feet of that descent the path swung right, then left again as it levelled out. And now I was walking along a narrow trail with steep wooded slopes climbing to my left, on my right a sheer drop over jagged rocky outcrops to the road far below.

I paused, braced, stared down. Europa Advance Road. A car was parked there, no sign of life. A red toy, rocking in the wind, glistening as if drenched in wet blood.

When I walked on, out in the open, the wind had the power of a giant hitting me repeated blows with a huge soft cushion carrying the weight of a dead elephant. It came in off the sea in fierce gusts, carrying with it driving rain smelling of salt spray. Battered, soaked, I was driven at an angle away from that sheer drop and forced to battle continually to avoid being thrown bodily against the wooded slope.

Ahead of me as I stumbled and staggered I saw the pathway once again narrow and twist its way into dense shrubbery that was soon clawing wetly at my clothes. There, as I slipped and almost fell where water tumbled boiling down the slope, I found myself some respite from the wind, and caught my breath. But it was a temporary lull. Once again the pathway widened and emerged from shelter into raw exposure. I pushed on, dashing the rain from my eyes, searching for Skaill and his son and beyond for any sign in the murk of Calum Wick and my Soldier Blue.

Suddenly I saw ahead of me a section of path that narrowed so much that safe walking was going to be almost impossible. The edge over the drop had broken away. Streaming flood water was causing more damage, breaking off muddy fragments. What remained for humans to stand on sloped severely to the right and was dangerously crumbling.

It was there that the man who had

summoned me was making his stand.

But it was a stand unlike anything I had imagined.

★ ★ ★

Nick Skaill was the one holding a gun. His knuckles were white with tension. Rainwater dripped from the pistol's barrel — it was almost a stream. If he pulled the trigger he'd either blow his father off the path, or reduce his own hand to bloody shreds.

He was standing back against the steep wooded slope that led to the naked rock high above, held there securely by the wind. His legs were slightly apart, braced against a muddy bank. He was as steady as the Rock itself.

Ronnie Skaill was not so fortunate. When he phoned me he must have been gazing fearfully into the barrel of the gun and following Nick's instructions. He'd been standing here ever since, held at gunpoint. He had his back to the drop and was visibly shaking. His heels were close to the crumbling edge. Instinctively he was leaning back into each fierce gust of wind, his eyes never moving from the gun aimed at his chest. As each gust abruptly died away he was left unbalanced, wobbling backwards, flapping his hands to avoid falling to his death.

I stopped when I saw them, ten yards away, a frozen tableau lashed by wind and rain. Time was running out for Ronnie Skaill. He must have known that his own cold-blooded murder was only minutes away. Leaning forward, legs bent, hands on knees as I looked for strength and inspiration, I was too far away to save him and his precarious position left him no room to move or help himself.

'Don't come any closer,' Nick said, grinning at me and waggling the gun. 'An' don't try to run away. You do, I'll shoot you in the back.'

'Like you shot Greenoak?'

'Yeah. And that clever dick of a cop, Haggard, him with his theories that were gettin' too close to the truth.'

'But that's not all, is it?'

'It's not all, and it's not over.' And now he was looking at his father, and the grin had twisted into a grimace of hate. 'Big-time Ronnie Skaill's goin' down, the big drop — '

'Why?'

That was Ronnie. He was weakening, I could see it. His voice was a croak. His eyes were scrunched up, fixed on his son, and it was hard to say if his cheeks were wet with tears, or with rain.

'Because you started it,' Nick said. 'An' where you went, we followed, up the stairs an' into bed, an' then everything went to pot because — '

'She couldn't take any more, Amanda,' I said. 'You'd taken over where your father left off and that was too much and she confided in somebody and that somebody told her there was only one way out and she was going to take it — '

'You, not we,' Ronnie Skaill moaned. He hadn't heard a word I'd said, and he was shaking his head, and now I could see, clearly, that he was crying. 'You said we, Nick, but it was you, just you, not Terry — '

He broke off as Nick threw back his head and laughed, laughter that bore the ring of madness before it was snatched away by the wind.

'Wrong. So fuckin' wrong. Who d'you think's down there now, in that car? Terry. Waitin' till this is over, finished. Then it's Catalan Bay for both of us, a boat there waitin', the Spanish coast no more than a mile away — '

'Not Terry, no, he wouldn't — '

'Fuckin' would. It was always Terry. Leadin' the way. Droppin' us both in the shit time and again, then gettin' me to do the dirty work to extract us. The trouble with Amanda started with Greenoak. Somehow, here in Gib, he found out what was goin' on and was about to bubble us.' He looked dispassionately at Ronnie. 'Probably found out from you, yeah? Took one look the first time you sashayed into Lagoon Deep with a flowered shirt and too-tight jeans and had you sussed straight off.'

I thought I heard a soft wail from Ronnie. It could have been the wind. His eyes were tight shut, his teeth clenched. And then I heard a stone, somewhere, rattling down the hillside, and my skin prickled.

'Then Amanda told Terry it was over,' Nick went on, 'and he knew there was no way she'd keep her mouth shut. So he gave his usual fuckin' orders and I was off, *jawohl, mein fuhrer*, your wish is my fuckin' command, and when I took a flight to the UK her days were numbered . . .'

He carried on in that vein, his tone now matter-of-fact, using the fingers of his free hand to list his victims as he came to them — Greenoak, Amanda, Tommy Mack, Harry Haggard — and in the storm his words were plucked from his lips by the wind, rising and falling like bad radio reception, but by then I'd tuned out anyway and my heart was pounding, the adrenaline rush causing a ringing in my ears.

For, beyond Nick and Ronnie, I could now see Calum and Sian. They were half walking, half stumbling down a treacherous, twisting slope — at least forty yards away. One of them must have kicked the loose stone, sent it over the edge — that's what I had heard. The rain was a translucent sweep of swirling grey through which they appeared as ghostly shapes. But it was slackening. The storm was dying. I saw Calum lift his hand, a signal that meant he'd seen us but gave no clue to his intentions.

The insistent moan of the wind drowned any sound they made as they picked their way gingerly down the rutted, streaming track towards the two Skaills.

Then Nick Skaill reached the end of his diatribe. Shaking the water from the pistol's cold steel as he pushed himself away from the muddy bank, he dashed the rain from his eyes and sent a look in my direction, loaded with menace. Then, probably without conscious thought, he turned his head and looked up the trail.

# 29

The wind finally did what it had been threatening and tore the thinning clouds apart. Suddenly I was gazing on a scene of almost Biblical beauty. The rain had eased. Like jewels scattered by a giant hand or fireflies as numerous as locusts, sparkling droplets seemed to float in the air. A brilliant shaft of sunlight lanced at Nick Skaill and he lifted a hand to shield his eyes. The dull metal pistol in his other hand, swinging once again towards his father, was turned into a weapon of solid silver by the dazzling light.

Ronnie Skaill's scream was one of pure terror. He knew he was going to take a bullet, but could make no sudden movement to save himself. Couldn't — but tried. He lunged at Nick, both hands claws that could seize nothing but thin air. The laws of physics were his undoing: every action has an opposite and equal reaction. To lunge, his back foot thrust down with his full weight, and he was betrayed by the wet, crumbling edge. A chunk broke off. Ronnie's foot slipped. As his leg dropped into space, he began to fall backwards. Desperately, he threw himself sideways. He landed half on, half off the path. His fingers clawed at loose, wet ground. With a wail, he began to slide.

Nick was standing with bent knees, holding the pistol with both hands. His eyes were wide, his face contorted with frustration: his father was about to die, and it was not Nick's doing. Hurriedly, he squeezed the trigger. The bullet winged harmlessly into the void. Screaming his frustration, he swung the gun to follow the crawling, scrabbling, sliding figure — and fired a second shot.

Blood blossomed like a red flower in the centre of Ronnie Skaill's white face. The bullet finished what he had started. His attempts to cling to the path, and to life, had been in vain. When the bullet hit him, he was already falling, his fingernails scraping deep gouges in the mud. He died instantly. His eyes rolled back in his head. Then he'd gone. All that was left were scars on the wet path, the snapping of branches as he plummeted limp and unfeeling down that 200 foot drop, the distant clatter of yet more falling rock.

Seconds. Perhaps fractions. That's all it had taken. Calum had broken into a jog, then a flat out sprint. When Nick fired the first shot, I launched myself at him. I heard him scream, then he fired his second, watched the bullet hit home and his father disappear from sight. Out of the corner of his eye he saw me charge, saw me winding up to swing a punch. Stepping back from the crumbling edge, he lashed out, back-handed. The pistol hit me on the bridge of the nose. I heard the crack of breaking bone, went down with a crunching splash. On hands and knees, dripping thin skeins of blood, I watched Calum through streaming eyes. His long legs had eaten up the ground. Ten yards, five yards, and he was damn near close enough to lunge for Nick's throat when the bullet hit him.

Nick stepped sideways, a matador letting the bull's weight carry him past. I heard Calum grunt. Beyond them, Sian was coming on more slowly. Calum's doing: I could imagine his words, 'leave it to me'. Weakly, I held up my hand.

'Stay back. Stay . . . '

The words bubbled, caught thickly in my throat. She didn't hear — couldn't hear — but there was nothing she could do. I watched in horror as Calum lurched sideways, his knees buckling. Then he went down with a splash, and slid over the edge.

Now Sian was running. Wet blonde hair flying, blue eyes flashing in the bright sunlight, she ran at Nick Skaill. But the bastard was laughing. He waited until she was so close he couldn't miss, then he drew back

301

his arm and flung the pistol. It hit her in the face. I heard the crack, saw her fold at the waist and half crouch with her head in her hands.

And with one final glance at the carnage, Nick Skaill stepped over the edge. He was there, then gone, his mocking laugh swiftly faded.

Then Sian had reached me. Head turned, straining to see to where Calum had gone over she was bending, clutching my shoulder, shaking me. Her cheekbone was red and swelling, her left eye already beginning to close.

'Calum,' she gasped, 'he's fallen, we've got to . . . '

She released me and was moving as she spoke. Almost tripping, she kicked up mud and stones as she stumbled to the very edge of the narrow path.

'Sian, no!'

I came up off my knees, lunged and grabbed her arm, swung her away from danger. She struggled, turned on me — this time noticed the blood, my ruined nose. She bit her lip. Her eyes were brimming.

'Jack, move yourself, that bastard shot his father, Calum, all three of them have gone over the bloody edge — '

'Ronnie's dead, Nick's getting away, he

planned it, there's a car waiting and there must be a way down —'

'Then go after him, leave Calum to me.'

'No! Nick's away, there's no catching him and Calum's too heavy for you.'

'Yes, and while we're talking he's dying.'

'Phone Romero.' With shaking hand I dug out my mobile and pressed it into her hand. 'Tell him Nick and Terry Skaill are driving from Europa to Catalan Bay, tell him there's a boat waiting . . .'

I was moving while talking. The sun was hot again, the wind had eased and the clouds were moving east leaving endless clear blue skies. I heard the bleep of the phone, Sian's voice, cool now, clear. I closed my eyes. Then, hardly daring to look, I stepped as close to the edge as I dared and peered down.

Calum was ten feet down a vertical drop, caught like a hooked worm by a thin, stunted tree that had probably been clinging to the same rock face when the British invaded in 1704. He was lying across the gnarled trunk like an old-time straddle high jumper who'd got the red flag. The tree was bent like a split cane rod fighting a big fish. I could hear an ominous crackling. Where the roots clung to the rock, fragments of stone were trickling from shallow fissures.

The tree dropped six inches. Calum

rocked. He took his eyes from roots that were slowly tearing loose as he watched, and squinted up at me with fire in his eyes and a look on his bearded face of withering scorn.

'I've been watching him,' he said, 'that Nick Skaill. He went down like a mountain goat, and all you two could do was stand up there arguing about which it was to be, him or me. What did you do to decide, toss a bloody coin?'

I looked at the blood soaking his shoulder and trickling from his fingers to fall in bright red droplets into the open space over which he hung.

'If we had, and I'd won,' I said, 'I'd be halfway home by now.'

'Typical.' He adjusted his position on the drooping tree, dislodging more crumbling rock. 'I don't know if you've noticed,' he said, 'but you appear to have a slight nosebleed.'

# 30

## Sunday

'If your nose really was broken,' Calum said, 'your face would be in a splint.'

'If you really had been shot,' I said, 'you'd be in hospital on a drip.'

'The obvious riposte being that instead of *on* one I'm sitting here *with* — '

'Don't say it,' Sian said, glaring at both of us in turn with her one good eye. 'Jack may be a lot of things but he's not that. And could I ask you both, please, to stop acting like a couple of soft kids? At least one of us was close to *death* out there on those bloody Mediterranean Steps.'

'In a force nine summer gale, torrential rain, soaked through, slipping and sliding in slick mud on the edge of a precipice.' I grinned painfully. 'Considering the circumstances, Soldier Blue, soft is a word that should have no place in your vocabulary.'

'The us being all *three* of us,' she pointed out, 'of whom I'm the only one to emerge with dignity, a sense of perspective, and a mature conviction that we were all bloody lucky.'

'Aye, well, as I was the one close to death I'll drink to that,' Calum said, and he picked up his orange juice and winked at me as he knocked it back.

He was using his left hand to hold his glass as his right arm was in a broad white sling, his usual loose-limbed sprawl replaced by stiffness as he favoured the shoulder that had taken Nick Skaill's bullet. When we'd woken that morning I'd solemnly accused Sian of being two-faced, and when she peered at her reflection in the mirror she couldn't deny it: the right side of her face was unmarked, but her left cheekbone was badly bruised, her eye swollen shut, the skin a shiny purple that, she said, reminded her of a Victoria plum. Me? Well, yes, despite Calum's scoffing, my nose really was broken — though the advice from the hospital was very little treatment necessary, don't hit any more fists or guns with my nose, and for the next few days keep in place the stylish gauze packing that was sticking rather attractively out of both nostrils.

Earlier, sitting in the shade of the pink polka-dot parasol, I'd spoken on the phone to Romero while Sian was in the shower and Calum prepared breakfast with one hand. Sian's desperate phone call from the Med Steps while I rescued the dangling Scot had been acted upon with speed. The DI expressed his gratitude, tempered with admonition: I had been foolhardy; Nick Skaill had been their problem, not mine, and I should have phoned at the very outset of the drama not at the end when it was almost too late.

'That aside,' he said, 'Ronnie Skaill's body was recovered, and in the other matter my men were successful. It was all very easy. Nick Skaill suffered a badly sprained ankle on the way down so was slow getting to the car. Pursuers and pursued arrived at Catalan Bay at almost the same time. Terry was helping Nick limp towards the waiting vessel when they were arrested.'

'That's all very well,' Sian said now, when I'd finished relating the conversation, 'but arresting is one thing, making a charge stick might not be so easy. Oh, I know,' she said, 'you'll testify and thanks to Tim they've got the gun and so on, but that's all to do with crimes committed here in Gibraltar. What about the one we're interested in? The fairground murders. Are you going to be able to clear Tim's name?'

'Romero has also spoken on the phone to Mike Haggard. Haggard told him that head hairs were found on Amanda Skaill that did not belong to the young lady. The theory is that Nick Skaill got close to her, perhaps

307

embraced her to deceive her into believing everything was hunky dory.'

Calum nodded his satisfaction. 'And the wonders of DNA will do the rest.'

He was quiet for a moment. We all were. Savouring success stumbled upon rather than achieved. Licking our wounds. Looking ahead to . . . what, exactly?

As always, Calum caught my mood.

'So, what about you two beauties?'

'Explain, Calum,' Sian said, looking at me in a way that made it clear no explanation was necessary but she wanted to hear what our wise friend had to say.

'Your business, which is not much more than two names on headed notepaper, is disappearing down the plughole. Satisfaction with your lot in this sun-soaked Mediterranean paradise is diminishing day by jolly-old day. You miss ice-cold Blighty, and all who sail in her stormy seas. There is surely only one decision to make — but have you got the bottle?'

'Succinctly put?' I said to Sian. 'Hit the nail on the head?'

'Accurately, and with force. We've already discussed it anyway — '

'But reached no conclusions.'

'So what we needed was a kick up the backside.'

'Duly delivered,' Calum said. 'And so . . . ?

'If a move requires bottle,' I said, 'it would help if it was a bottle full of money. As we found when we set up shop here, moves are expensive.'

'In that case,' Calum said, 'help is at hand.'

I stared. 'It is?'

'But of course. Remember we talked about wee Stan Jones and his complicated mathematical system?'

I groaned. Sian looked puzzled. Calum pressed on.

'Well, you're not the only one here who can make an early morning phone call, and I happen to know that there's a hundred to one shot running at some godforsaken track on the other side of the world . . . '

He went on, but I'd blanked him out. I was too busy watching Sian. She was listening, but looking at me. She shrugged, and rolled her one visible eye. But I couldn't help noticing, with one of those delicious tingles she invariably evokes in me, that on the undamaged side of her face there was a definite flush of excitement.